CW00516569

MONKSHOOD

Daniel Mullaney

1

The wood splintered as he pushed with all he had. The sash window budged an inch with each heave, the blisters of white paint popping. There was a chill outside but the room needed to breathe. As a breeze let itself in it flushed some moldered air out. Asthma was one ailment that Finn didn't have, but as the heavy, damp air filled his lungs he felt a sensation he could only equate - from experience - to the rearing of a mild panic attack.

The room was old, wooden and often described as quaint. Finn Shelton didn't find it quaint, he saw only the potential for splinters. The motes of mould dancing freely in the air, waiting for his next inhale. The warm, breeding grounds of ticks, mites and other bloodsuckers. Hoards of parasites waiting for him to touch a surface, take a seat or lay his head on a cushion.

Finn held his head outside the window and took in his surroundings; The cobbled streets, the jaunty slate roofs, swinging shop signs, a steeple protruding from the far end of the village, and all around, moors, as far as his eyes could see. He noticed the clouds, sweeping the hills, defined and ominously grey. He squinted and tried to make out a sea view, which was promised to him in a brochure. He couldn't tell if he was looking at a far off shore or the base of a breaking blue sky. Maybe if the miasma would clear, he'd spot the white spec of a crashing wave.

Heavy footsteps, and the teeth gritting slam of an antique door demanded Finn's attention.

'What d'ya think?' Bellowed Rufus Granville as he dropped his bags to the floor.

Finn - so delicate in everything he did - couldn't help but wince as his friend thundered across the oak floorboards, his large limbs swinging close to the old furniture and trinkets.

The pair couldn't be more different. Finn; pale and fair haired, a morsel of a man. His stringy limbs hung from his torso like a whirling drum. Rufus; Dark and well groomed, held himself proudly. His broadness married an assertive gait, and to those who didn't know him, he was intimidating. Finn knew him, and over the years, their friendship had tested Rufus' tolerance. There seemed to be no boundaries to his patience for Finn's constant ineptness.

'It's going to rain.' Said Finn.

He moved away from the window and sat on the edge of his bed, still wary of bed bugs.

'It *is* September. And this *is* Cornwall. What did you expect?' Explained Rufus.

'It's just my luck.'

'And what about my luck? I'm here too, you don't hear me complaining.'

He had a point. Rufus swung his heaviest bag onto his mattress, as it landed a ring of dust rose into the air.

'Quaint.' He said, with a smile on his face.

Finn squinted his eyes and shook his head, he exaggerated the action for his friends benefit.

'Ah come on, this is what you wanted, a bit of history.' Said Rufus as he outstretched his arms and scanned the room. '*I* wanted to go to Newquay. *I* wanted to try my hand at a bit of surfing, and maybe, just maybe get my leg over. You wanted this, and being the great guy that I am, I agreed to it. I even drove for six hours to get you here!'

'I'm grateful, really I am. It's just that, now that I'm here, it all looks a bit, well…a bit shit!'

'I think it's nice. Anyway, there's a pub, if all else fails we can get pissed.'

Rufus tried his best to cheer up Finn but it didn't seem to matter. Stubborn in his own melancholy way, Finn wouldn't budge.

'Did you see that girl in reception?' Asked Rufus, trying a new tactic.

'What, the hotel owner? The old woman stinking of seashells?'

'No! The top heavy girl who checked in before us, she had a friend, and in a place like this there can't be much competition, eh?' Rufus winked.

Finn screwed up his face.

'Oh right, because if there was even the slightest competition, I wouldn't stand a chance, is that what you mean.' Finn knew that this was not what he meant, but he did enjoy a little sympathy.

'Hey, we can't all look like me!' Rufus turned to a mirror opposite his bed and smiled. His teeth perfectly straight and impeccably white.

Rufus had decided not to mollify him, and Finn felt that his friend had become wise to his tactics. Finn had always told himself that he had the superior intellect. If nothing else, he had that. Lately he had been questioning himself, and his capabilities as a thinker. This was one of the reasons he needed to get away.

'Do you hear that?' Said Rufus.

Before Finn could answer, Rufus had glided to the far wall, and in one sleek motion pressed his ear to it.

'What are you doing?' Asked Finn, standing up from the overly firm mattress.

Rufus hushed his friend and narrowed his eyes as if to concentrate.

'They're next door!' Rufus whispered. '*Jugs*, and her friend are in the next room!'

A childish smirk appeared on his face as he jerked with giddy excitement. Finn had witnessed this before. He would behave this way on a regular basis, whenever potential mates were on his radar. Rufus snorted at the plaster, implying that the females were so close that he could smell them. In actual fact, he received a nostril full of dust and a sudden sneezing fit that sent him away from the wall, and stumbling back to his bed.

'Did you hear that?'

'What?' Grunted Jessica, preoccupied with her laptop.

'A *manly* sneeze!' Jested Stacey, smiling from ear to ear.

'No wifi, not one flippin' bar!'

'They're next door.'

'Who is?' Asked Jess, shaking her laptop as if to damn it.

'Those guys from downstairs,' Stacey explained 'you know, the big black guy and his wee friend.' She parodied them with a brief charade. 'You know!' With her chest out and arms fixed at rigid angles she posed as Rufus. And for Finn, she performed a simple hand gesture; her finger and thumb held an inch apart, which she concluded with a hearty chuckle.

'There's no internet here, the website clearly stated wifi, free with accommodation.' Jess stood up and looked at the ceiling. 'This, is, bollocks!'

'Calm down. We didn't come here to surf the bloody internet. We're on holiday. Aren't we? We should be doing some actual surfing, you know, with waves and stuff. In the *real* world.'

'You're on holiday. I'm here to work.'

Jess fell limply onto her bed, arms outstretched.

'Why ever else would we be visiting *Golgothaan*? A shitty little village, in the middle of nowhere. I'm just trying to make the most of it.' Said Stacey as she fell onto her own bed, parallel to her friends. She rolled onto her side to face Jess. 'We are gonna have some fun aren't we? Tell me we're gonna have some fun.'

'Yes, yes. We are gonna have some fun.' Exhaled Jess, defeated. 'But I need to do some research, and you'll just have to find something, or *someone* else to do.' She smiled, and both of them giggled.

Jessica Brady knew how to cater to her friends overactive sex drive. She would instill the prospect of a sexual encounter to her, the same way a parent would silence a child with the promise of a sweet, or a toy. Jess longed for a fling or two of her own, but they didn't come to her as easily as they did to Stacey. Even when they did, she would dismiss them, thanks to a mix of paranoia and stubbornness. She wasn't going to be second best and with Stacey around, she always was.

Stacey Garland had what most men were looking for; curves. Breasts that threatened to break free of ill-fitting shirts, and low cut vests. Crescents in all the right places, and even her mahogany hair was voluptuous, rarely a strand out of place. Jessica on the other hand struggled to fill a bra. She was athletic enough, slender and tall, with legs Stacey would often claim to envy, but her lackluster dress sense and negativity would deter most advances.

'The fun shall begin tonight. The pub methinks, and I won't take no for an answer.'

Jessica met Stacey's determined eyes and found it hard to resist. Eventually she succumb with a gentle nod, much to her fun loving friends relief.

The Scarlet Lodge had not been this busy in years. The first to check in was Eugene Mire. He was also the first to unpack, the first to freshen up and the first to explore the village. The rain couldn't hinder his well laid schedule. Waterproofed and airtight in matching anorak and Wellington boots, he took to the cobbles like a bloodhound.

To watch Eugene you would think he was in a hurry, pacing to some appointment that couldn't wait. This wasn't true, everything could wait, everything but Eugene. Father Time had kept up with this tourist though, right down to the cracked skin and thinning hair. His eyes required thick spectacles and his ears, a hearing aid at full volume. His left hip had been ground to chalk dust over the years and yet he never let this falter his pace.

Hiking was his passion, and the Golgothaan Moors were perfect for such an enthusiast. Eugene would walk from village to village, and take in the sights along the way. This was the first stop on his trail, a pilgrimage to commemorate his wife's passing a few years prior. Ethel loved to hike, maybe even more than Eugene.

Eugene passed by everything that Golgothaan Village had to offer, glancing the buildings as if to take mental snapshots. Nostalgia struck as he peered into a butcher's shop window; the sawdust on the floor, the brown paper, the chalkboards. All of this distracted him as he took an uneasy step. His foot slipped from under him. He didn't fall - he was an accomplished walker and sure-footing was a talent - he'd just lost his stride for a moment.

Steadied now, Eugene noticed a brass plate, embedded in the cobblestones. Wet from the rain, it mimicked ice. *Emelia Staunt, murdered on this spot, 1909* the engraving read, as Eugene knelt in for closer inspection, holding his glasses to the bridge of his nose to prevent them from sliding off. He had seen plaques like this before, usually in taverns or inns, and usually to mark the death of someone of notoriety. He didn't recognise the name, but then he didn't know everything, though he would never admit this.

There were six more plates - that he noticed - on his journey to the only tavern in town. Each plate was an unfamiliar name, and each either claimed that a murder had occurred or a body had been found.

The Ashen Maid tavern, according to the guide book that nestled in Eugene's breast pocket, was the third structure to be erected in Golgothaan. The first was the church and the second was the Scarlet Lodge.

'Just the one.' He promised himself as he stood by the taverns tiny oak door. It hid under a jaunty eave, and written across the most prominent beam was the words *Mind your head*. Eugene checked his watch, checked the sky and then sidled through the doorway, gingerly tucking his chin into his chest until he was well clear of the beam overhead.

It rained intermittently, coating the cobbled streets in a glaze that blinded when the sun found room to shine. Finn and Rufus were dressed, reeking of cologne and ready to leave. They had been for hours now. The evening drew ever closer and Rufus had decided that it was now or never. Overly familiar with their lodgings, it was time to leave. Fresh air beckoned, and as they stepped onto the damp street a chilling breeze almost ushered Finn back inside.

'Come on, at least its downhill.' Said Rufus, feeling like he had to drag his friend down the road. 'Just follow the water.'

Rivulets of rainwater poured down the street, flowing towards the tavern and guiding the duo's way. Drainage seemed to be a problem here, and Finn feared that they would arrive at a lake, where the tavern once stood. The village didn't offer many sights, but Finn appreciated its charm, likening the scenery to that of a role-playing video game he would often enjoy; in secret of course. It was a short walk to the Ashen Maid, and a relief to be escaping the bitter damp air.

The warmth of burning logs extended an invitation as Rufus opened the front door. This with the décor of warped wood - adorned with brass paraphernalia and horse shoes - and rich claret walls epitomized what the pair imagined a true country tavern to be. The bar was clear of crowds, with only a few locals propping it up, and tables tucked into every crevice. There must have been a seat for every Golgothaan resident if needed with some left over, though it was hard to imagine the pub ever being full.

Rufus pointed to a table and then asked 'What're you having?'. Finn said what he'd always say, 'Beer' and then lurked over to the corner that was picked out for him. He sat with his back to the wall and scanned the room. A handful of rural types sat, melancholically gulping house ales and bitters. Most of the men wore flat caps and tweed, and some had the company of their wives; stern and stout with faces as warped as the woodwork. Finn imagined a hostile glare from the locals, but to his surprise they seemed indifferent. Probably used to tourists by now? He thought. At a lonelier, gloomier end of the bar sat someone foreign to Golgothaan. His bright anorak and overstocked backpack gave him away. The man seemed drunk, barely holding up his own head to talk to whoever it was that served him behind the bar.

Rufus slammed two pints of beer on the table, spilling a little and demanding Finn's attention.

'Have you seen the talent in here?' Asked Rufus wryly.

'By the looks of it, they're all taken.'

'More's the pity.'

The pair, chuckled discretely as they checked for eavesdroppers.

'Well, what do you think?' Asked Rufus.

Finn took another look around, 'It's nice. I like it.'

Rufus checked his friends face for irony, but to his surprise, he seemed genuinely impressed.

'Really? Well, I'm glad you like it, *I suppose.* A little dire isn't it? What this place needs a jukebox. And maybe a bit of eye' Before he could finish, the tavern door opened. 'candy!'

It must have started raining again. The last two guests of the Scarlet Lodge entered, shaking droplets loose from their jackets.

'Speak of the devil.' Said Finn, noticing Rufus' eyes light up.

'They're all wet!' Muttered Rufus, instantly realising the crudeness of his statement. This brought a smile to his face.

'I'm not going over, I don't care what you say, I just want to sit here and enjoy my pint!' Finn reinforced this with a gulp of beer, followed by a satisfied exhale.

'They're here.' Whispered Stacey.

'So they are.' Replied a disinterested Jessica as she hung her jacket on the back of a chair.

The pair sat, Stacey ensuring that she had the best seat to view of Rufus' table. She kept watch but had an amazing talent for appearing blasé, whenever she felt eyes upon her she would turn her head and become uncommonly prudish. Jessica was truly indifferent, resigned to forever being the wallflower. Tonight, next to Stacey's proudly displayed cleavage, she didn't stand a chance, experience had taught her as much.

Despite her overshadowing, she was generous. Generous or careless? Jessica would often question. Money was a trivial concept to Stacey, her father paying for the round of drinks that she now ordered at the bar. He'd paid for her expensive clothes, her car, her tiny expensive dog that he was now looking after. Even the holiday that the pair were now trying to enjoy. Jessica took advantage of this, much like Stacey did her father.

As she stood at the bar, she held herself in a well rehearsed way. She ensured that her dress rode up, just enough. Straightened her back until her bust cast a shadow over the bar. Jessica watched, knowing her friend only too well, and every time it made her smile and shake her head discretely. Drinks in hand she returned to the table, and as she placed them down Jessica waited for the obligatory, and exaggerated arching of the back. She made sure that the boys could see as her dress hung from her chest, leaving little to the imagination.

'You do make me laugh!' Chuckled Jessica.

'Why?'

'You know why. The act, it's always the same.'

'I have no idea what you're talking about?' Smiled Stacey as she sat down.

'You're shameless,' Jessica nodded to the boy's table 'he's nothing special.'

'What are you talking about? Look at those arms! Those shoulders!'

'Not my type.'

Stacey examined her friend.

'Oh I get it.'

'What?' Snapped Jessica.

'It's because he's black!'

Stacey's face froze, her mouth in the shape of a comical 'O'. Jessica appeared deeply offended.

'It's not that at all!'

'Yes it is, I know you Jessica, you're a racist!'

Jessica held her breath, checked the coast and then leant in towards her accuser.

'Keep your voice down!' She whispered. 'I'm nothing of the sort, you can't say stuff like that!'

'Yes I can, Racist.' Stacey laughed, regressing to a childlike state. 'I just don't find *black* men attractive, same as you might not like blonde hair, or short guys! It's the same thing!'

'Oh so you don't like Brown skin?'

'That's not what I said, and you know it!'

Jessica began to get agitated, it was clear for all to see, yet Stacey continued to tease her, as she often would.

'Yes it is, you said that you don't like black people!'

'No, I didn't' Jessica growled. 'Stop this now, I've had enough!'

'Okay, okay. Calm down,' Stacey held a smirk, 'Racist!'

'Who's a racist?' Came a male's voice.

During their quarrel, Rufus had made his way to the bar, picking the part closest to Stacey's table. He wore a grin as he half turned to face them.

'No one, no one's a racist!' Blurted Jessica.

'Oh I do hope not, I had had such high hopes for tonight.'

His reply was to the table, but his eyes were on Stacey.

'We were having a private conversation, are you always so rude?' Said Stacey.

'No, not always. Not in public anyway.'

Rufus remained fixed on Stacey, Jessica darting between the pair rolled her eyes, knowing that anything she did now would go unnoticed. The tavern owner slid two drinks to Rufus demanding his attention with a subtle cough.

'Well, despite my rudeness, and your standing on certain ethnicities, my friend and I would like to invite you to our table.'

'We aren't racist!' Insisted Jessica 'You must have misheard.'

'Ha, it's okay. I'm only joking, I believe you. The offer stands, and I hope to see *you* shortly.'

He smiled his most charming smile, teeth and all. It was obvious that the invitation was for Stacey, and extended to Jessica only as a courtesy. But she was used to this and no matter how much of a fight she would put up, Stacey would win. They had learned to bypass the arguments altogether now and just go with what Stacey would decide to do.

'Maybe. Don't hold your breath.' Said Stacey, as she showed him her back. Taking a sip from her drink she grinned at Jessica, remaining there until Rufus had hesitantly drifted back to his table.

One drink had become four, and no matter how much he insisted, the figure behind the bar would refuse his money. 'On the house!' He would say. Eugene had passed his threshold, and his spinning head was testament to it. Three was usually his limit, but as he finished his fourth he craved another. The sun had set, and the moors were too dark to explore now. His backpack was on the floor and his anorak unzipped.

'Same again.' He requested.

The man behind the dark corner of the bar seemed to remain by Eugene's side, his own personal bar steward, whose intention seemed to be just one thing; to get his customer well and truly blotto.

'On the house.' Said the barman, as he waved away Eugene's cash filled hand. He insisted, firmly each time, as if to gain favour from the hiker. Something he could redeem when least expected.

'My wife. She never liked a drink.' Said Eugene as he examined the ale below his chin.

'Is that right?' Said the barman, his voice hushed.

'Yes, god rest her soul. I loved her so much, have I told you that?'

'Yes, yes you have.'

Eugene really had, many times. The barman's patience was commendable.

'She was supposed to be here, this was for her. It *is* for her.' Eugene sniffed as he took another gulp. 'She's with me, every step of the way. I'm sure of it!'

Eugene looked up, half expecting to see her ethereal form above him. Validating his superstitions.

'I'm sure she is.' Said the shadow behind the bar.

'I know she is. She has to be.'

What had started with sips, had now become swigs, and it wasn't long before he had necked his fifth pint of house ale. This was it, his limit, his wavering consciousness assured him of this. He dropped his glass, that rolled to the edge of the bar. The barman caught it before it was sure to shatter on the floor. He did this to keep their moment discreet, their existence obscured from the others, and at this dark, murky end of the tavern, it was easy enough to do.

'I'm done!' Blurted Eugene.

'Yes, I suppose you are.' Said the bar steward as he watched Eugene's head bob up and down as though it were hanging by a piece of elastic.

As his vision blurred the grain of the wood on the bar, he shook his head. He noticed a small white shape slide across the counter, and it rested under his nose. It was a book of matches, white with *The Ashen Maid* printed on it.

'These are for you.' Said the shadowy figure.

'Don't smoke!' Exclaimed Eugene, 'I quit.'

'Take it, it's yours.'

Eugene held his head up at great effort. He tried to find the bar steward's eyes, but his focus denied it. He nodded his head and grabbed the book with all the grace of an ape clasping food. He didn't know why, but for some reason he felt obliged. Placing them in his anorak pocket he then slapped his hands on the bar.

'That's it friend. Calling it a night.' He slurred.

'The night is young Eugene.'

As he said his name, Eugene ruffled his brow. He couldn't remember telling the bar steward his name. Deciding he must have at some point in his drunken state.

'Ethel was promised a hike. She wants to see the moors. You wouldn't want to disappoint her now would you?'

The bar steward's tone had changed, it was seductive, and Eugene had begun to feel influenced.

'I did promise her.' Eugene slapped his forehead. 'One drink! One drink I said! Forgive me Ethel.'

He slapped his head again, violently so, before cradling it in his arms. He let out a tear or two, followed by a snort. He'd always been a gloomy drunk. The shadow leant in.

'It's not too late Eugene. The moors are peaceful at night, the stars are bright here. They will guide your way, the moon will reveal your path.'

Eugene examined his new friend, steadied himself and contemplated his words.

'You're right.' He said as he struggled to lift his backpack. 'Ethel would want this.'

He stood up, his footing delicate, and swung his pack onto his shoulders sending him forward into the bar under the weight.

'Follow your nose Eugene, you'll know what to do.' Whispered the figure, before drifting away from the bar and the hiker.

Finn noticed the drunken rambler as he clambered out of the tavern. It was comical to watch, and he would usually have brought it to Rufus' attention but he was much too preoccupied. Jessica and Stacey had made themselves at home on their table, and as per usual, Rufus had claimed the prettiest girl as his own. Joviality and flirtation ruled one end of the table, Rufus and Stacey conversing with rarely a breath taken. Jessica and Finn sat silently at the other end, slurping their drinks in the hope to become drunk, and in turn uninhibited.

'So what brings you two to Golgothaan?' Asked Finn.

'Well, I'm here to do some research.' Answered Jessica.

'Oh really? That's interesting,' It wasn't but he thought he'd make an effort. 'What kind of research?'

Jessica turned to face him, she loved to talk about her work.

'I'm a history student, and this place holds more than its share.'

'Is that right?'

'Yeah, if you were to look at this place, the village, those who know would swear to it being built in the eleventh century. The architecture is typical of that time, but records claim that this is untrue.' She caught her breath.

'Oh really?' Said Finn as his interest rose. He turned to meet her gaze.

'Absolutely,' She smiled, her excitement clear. 'These buildings, and indeed this very tavern are much, much newer.'

'How much?' Inquired Finn as he moved closer.

'Try eight or nine hundred years!'

Jessica sat back, satisfied with the reaction Finn gave as he stared wide eyed. He shook his head as if to make sense of it.

'But why? Why would it look like this? What's the point?'

Jessica leaned in once more, and whispered as if it were a secret.

'That's what I'm here to find out.'

The intimacy of her reply drew Finn's attention to her eyes. They were blue-green, and her eyeliner understated, just the way he liked it. Her smile was warm, teeth impeccable. Suddenly the night had become much more interesting, and as he gulped his drink he hoped that she would mirror him.

'What about you, why are you here?' Asked Jessica.

'No reason, we're on holiday if you can believe it?'

'Really? Why here? I thought people came to Cornwall for the beaches?'

'I really don't know. It looked nice in the brochure.'

'Golgothaan has a brochure?'

'Well it was more of a leaflet really.' Finn jested, coaxing a giggle from Jessica.

He turned to see his friend - who was now quiet - at the other end of the table.

'Well they seem to be enjoying themselves.'

Jessica acknowledged her friend with her arms around Rufus. They writhed as their tongues picked each other's mouth clean, their heads rolling dramatically. The scene made it uncomfortable for the reserved pair, who by now wished that they had the confidence to do the same.

The moors offered no cover as the wind howled across the plains. It brought with it a numbing chill, but Eugene endured. He scanned the clear night's sky, and marvelled at the countless stars, wondering how they could remain so still while the wind battered his bones so powerfully. The moon offered some light - as the bar steward had promised - but it's ambience highlighted the horizon and not much else.

Eugene, still numb from the house ales, stumbled clumsily, dragging his boots across matted clods of grass, occasionally falling under the weight of his pack. He was quick enough to resume his aimless wandering, climbing to his feet and using the momentum to move forward a little. The shady barman had given Eugene a task, and he felt obliged to carry it out. He wasn't sure why, but being as intoxicated as he was he felt exhausted even questioning it.

For some reason he head uphill for the most part. His calves burned and his lungs seemed to shrink, yet he persisted, feeling the wind grow stronger as he reached the peak. The wind seemed to whisper, and as aggressive as the gale was the voice it carried was gentle and calming. It was familiar to Eugene and it wasn't long before he realised whose voice it was. It was his wife, and whether it was real or not, he was in no state to question it, it gave him strength and that was what he needed right now.

'Ethel!' He yelled, choked by the wind.

Her whisper was fragmented, mingling with the howling wind, but it was undeniably her. Eugene could pick out words but it didn't make any sense. It warmed his heart nonetheless and he felt a tear blown across his cheek, making its way to his ear.

'Where are you?' He screamed as his pace quickened.

'Need…you…' Whispered the wind.

'I need you too my love, I miss you so…!'

He was cut short as he fell forward, confronted with an elaborate stack of logs and twigs. Damp and smelling of rot.

'What is this?' He asked.

The wind ignored his question.

'Is this it?' He cried. 'Is this why I'm here?'

The voice broke through the howling wind once more.

'…Eugene…my love…the fire…'

As fragmented as the soothing voice was, Eugene felt that he knew - and had somehow always known - what he was to do. He dropped his pack but still felt heavy. The matchbook in his pocket seemed to gain weight. He pulled it out and examined it, then he examined the stack of soaked wood at his feet. The logs had a purpose and the bartender had given him the matchbook for a reason. Before he could put two and two together, he was holding a lit match, the flame refusing to dance in the wind. It burned with ambition, and despite the futility of trying to ignite the saturated wood with a single match, Eugene bent his knees until it was within reach. It took a moment, as the flame touched the first splinter, the pyre roared to life. The wood squeaked and popped as the flames grew taller than Eugene stood. He backed off to save his eyebrows, the heat drying his wrinkled face.

'Is this it my love? Did I do right?' He yelled, looking towards the embers that rose in the nights sky.

There came no reply.

'Ethel? Speak to me!'

Still no reply, just the crackle of the fire.

'Don't leave me…' He whimpered.

He was utterly alone, he felt this and it sank his heart. Suddenly he was sober. Whatever it was that spoke to him in the wind was gone, and despite the warmth of the fire he felt the chill of the night more than before. It was hazy, his reasons for being on the moor, for lighting the pyre, for listening to the mysterious barman in the first place. He checked his surroundings, as if he'd just woken up in a strange place.

Lost now, he turned his watery eyes to the amber glow of Golgothaan, no larger than a penny on the black horizon. How did he make it this far, in this cold and this darkness? He thought to himself. His head throbbed, it was a pain that used to follow his drinking binges, a problem he'd dealt with a long time ago thanks to the love of his wife. He felt ashamed that all of his hard work had been lost thanks to the forked tongue of the shady barman, his words so manipulative, his ales so seductive. Eugene through all of his confusion felt a rage. The barman was going to answer his questions, just as soon as he could make the trek back into town.

The walk was arduous, harder than before, but a new momentum carried him. Anger was a great motivator. Eugene could only tell how far he'd travelled by turning occasionally to judge the size of the mysterious fire. Each time he'd sworn he'd walked further than he did but the flames didn't seem to shrink. Checking the fire one last time he noticed something; A silhouette moving across the glow, hiding the fire for a moment. It was a figure, and as soon as one passed another would follow. Eugene froze, watching what seemed to be a crowd circling the fire. He was alone a few minutes ago, he was sure of it, the horizon though dark, was straight for miles around. A gathering of people would have made a dent to the star-speckled skyline. The bodies moved yet made no sound, their movements unnatural and eerie. The pit of Eugene's stomach was telling him to go, to run back to town as fast as his old legs would carry him. Out here he had nothing but his instincts to go on, so he dropped his pack and ran.

Quite the gathering of glasses had found its way to their table. The tavern owner quick enough to serve up the drinks, but not up to scratch when it came to collecting the empties. It was a realisation to witness the spoils of the night, Finn convinced that this gulp would be his last. Rufus was in the bathroom, his fourth visit of the night, coincidentally, Stacey was away from the table also, nowhere to be seen.

Finn turned and squinted, focusing on Jessica's face, hoping to read her expression despite his inebriated state. She seemed to be smiling, even finding his state amusing as her smile widened.

'Having a good time?' She asked.

'Yesh,' He slurred 'What ab-about you?'

'Yes, surprisingly.'

'S-surprisingly?'

'Yeah, I didn't think I would. In fact, I didn't even want to come here.'

'Me neither, it was Rufus that dragged m-me here.'

Finn offered a smile that made him look like a sloth, the slow nodding of his head only added to the impression.

'I'm sorry, I ap-appear to have gotten myself a little dwunk!' He confessed.

'Don't apologise, you're on holiday. You're supposed to be drunk.'

Finn moved his hand across the table and after a small fumble, landed it atop of Jessica's.

'You're l-loverly, you know that?'

The statement seemed to offend her. She slipped her hand out from under his.

'No I'm not, Finn. You're just drunk.'

'Yes you are, you're b-beautiful.'

'I think it's time for bed, don't you?'

'Y-yes please! Let's go.' Blurted Finn, misinterpreting Jessica and accepting an invitation that was never there. He raised his eyebrows and had never looked so sleazy.

Whatever progress he had made with Jessica throughout the night was suddenly lost with those four words. He was back to square one.

'Alone, Finn. Go to bed… Alone!' Jessica scanned the tavern. 'Just as soon as the other two come back.'

The couple shared a few minutes of complete silence. Finn, now wounded, sat with his arms crossed and his face puckered. Jessica ignored him, feeling validated in her belief that all men are only ever after one thing. Her prudish morals often standing in the way of a good time, unlike her buxom friend Stacey. Jessica failed to see the compliment in it, instead explaining it away as the lack of options or the desperation of the other party. Her self-esteem was zero, whether Finn actually believed she was beautiful or not.

For Finn this wasn't the case. He liked her, and the more they spoke the more attractive she became. It wasn't the drink, but unfortunately for him his confidence rose with each pint until he was brimming over with it. Failing to see the line until he'd crossed it. It would always end this way for him.

A welcomed distraction came at the other end of the bar; Rufus and Stacey being nudged out of the male toilets and back onto the tavern floor. The short, stout, tavern owner was prodding a giggling Rufus, careful so as not to provoke the six foot four, broad shouldered black guy. He had a reputation to keep and a knack for making his blows appear harder than they actually were. Stacey was ahead of them, shaking her head, embarrassed and eager to return to her table. Her head was down as if it hid her somehow. Every old man in the pub had kept one eye on her since she had entered the

Ashen Maid. Careful so as not to be caught out by their mean looking spouses.

'You dirty so and so's! I don't know what you think this place is, this aint no bloody knocking shop. Ain't one of your grubby little night clubs!' Ranted the tavern owner, his voice cracked and higher than expected. 'This is a respectable place, we won't be having any of that here, do you understand, big man?'

The tavern owner was now safe behind the bar, gripping two lager taps and foaming slightly in the corners of his mouth. Rufus had wiped the smirk from his face, he could be quite reasonable at times.

'I'm sorry, I really am. I meant you no disrespect. This is a nice place, a nice village and it seems that the drink has got the better of me, that's all.' He explained in his most charming manner.

The owner examined Rufus, looking him up and down through a furrowed brow. He exhaled, slowly raising his eyebrows.

'Well, you seem to have manners, and I wouldn't want your stay here to be an unpleasant one. You and your friends can stay,' The owner pointed his finger at Rufus. 'but you better behave, I'm telling ya, we won't have it any other way, you hear me, young'un?'

The tavern owner scanned the faces in the seats, hoping that his threat had been heard and his reputation sustained.

'We will behave, sir.' Rufus nodded emphatically. 'You have my word.'

'Very good.' Said the owner as he sidled down the bar - chest inflated - to a waiting customer.

Rufus wandered back to his seat, his tail between his legs, an act for all that were watching.

'I think it's time to go.' Said Rufus as he dropped into his chair.

'I agree.' Breathed Jessica.

Finn shook his head.

'I wanna shtay, I'm having f-fun.' He mumbled.

'I think you've had enough, mate.' Said Rufus, smiling kindly.

'Y-you're one to talk, I know where you've been. The p-pair of ya!'

Stacey covered her smirk with her hand, looking at Rufus and then Jessica who seemed unimpressed.

'You couldn't wait?' whispered Jessica.

'I don't know what you're talking about?' Giggled Stacey.

'Look, it's been a good night,' Rufus placed his hand on Stacey's leg, discreetly under the table. 'a very good night, but I think the locals might turn if we outstay our welcome.'

'Ah, it's okay for you, you two are gonna f-find a nice shpot to fuck! What am I gonna do?' Asked Finn.

'You are gonna go to bed, mate. Sleep it off.' Explained Rufus as he got up and moved around the table. 'Give me a hand would ya?' He asked Jessica as they both held Finn's arms.

'What're you doin'?' He asked as they dragged him away from the table, his legs seemed to move towards the exit despite his protestations. 'I don't wanna…'

As the group made their way onto the street, the cold seemed to snap Finn back to life.

'I can walk, let me walk!' He barked as he shook himself free.

'Come on, mate. Let's not make a big thing out of this, eh?' Begged Rufus.

Finn stopped, took in a deep breath and then looked at his friend. The concern in Rufus' face was enough to convince him. He was a true friend.

'Let's go to bed.' Said Finn as he started making his way up hill.

The walk was much longer than it should have been. A drunken Finn could find distraction in anything. His ramblings were at the philosophical stage now, and as intelligent as he was, he wasn't making much sense.

They had arrived at the Scarlet Lodge and thankfully the front door was unlocked. It seemed that this was safe in such a tight knit community. The front desk was empty and a few lamps lit their way up the creaking stairs and to their rooms. The last thing Finn remembered was being helped into bed by Rufus. The bed bugs didn't seem to bother him anymore as he passed out atop the sheets.

Rufus, ever the gentleman, escorted the girls to their door. Deciding to linger outside in the hall as they sat on their beds, chatting.

'Why is he waiting there?' Whispered Jessica.

Stacey turned her head to acknowledge him and then turned back to her friend.

'We are gonna take a walk, have a chat, check out the village.'

'It's one in the morning!'

'If this was Newquay then the night would still be young. Why should Golgothaan be any different?'

Jessica moved her head closer to Stacey, ensuring that Rufus couldn't see her mouth.

'You don't even know him.'

'I never know them, but as far as they go he seems nice. Don't you think?'

'The murderers, the rapists, they *always* seem nice. That's how they get ya!'

'You're being ridiculous, I'm a grown woman, and you promised me some fun.' Stacey turned to check that her suitor was still standing by. 'Anyway, how did it go with the other guy?'

'Finn? Well he got drunk, he came on to me and I told him where to go. Same as always.'

'You're an idiot. He seemed nice enough, you two seemed to be getting on. You could be having some fun right now too but oh no, Sister Brady is above all that.' Stacey shook her head. 'Just what is it you want? Who are you waiting for, because I'm telling you right now, your standards aint ever gonna be met, girl.'

Jessica knew that her friend was right, but she didn't appreciate the truth. It touched a nerve and stung like most truths do.

'Your date is waiting, I'm going to sleep.' Snapped Jessica as she laid back and rolled onto her side.

Stacey didn't apologise, she didn't feel that she needed to. Jessica needed to hear it. She whispered 'Sweet dreams' before standing up and meeting a smiling Rufus in the hall. She checked on her unmoving friend one last time before closing the door.

The silence was something they couldn't get used too. You would expect crickets or the distant crashing of waves, but no. The Golgothaan moors surrounded the village and the terrain, as wide as it was, wasn't much of a habitat. The grass was short and lifeless and the sea miles away, despite the promise of it in the brochure. The residents - all forty-seven of them - were fast asleep and even the

Ashen Maid had settled for the night. It seemed that the town had died when the foursome had made their way back to the lodge.

Rufus and Stacey walked the cobbles arm in arm. Clambering and flirtatiously patting each other. They were overly aware of just how far their whispers and footsteps carried in the empty street. But it was peaceful enough, and in a way romantic; They felt like the last two people on earth.

'This is nice.' Whispered Stacey.

'This? I didn't think *this* was your scene. I know it's not mine.'

'Maybe it's the company?'

'Well if it's anything, it's probably the company.'

'Bit full of yourself ain't ya?' She jested.

'Coming from you woman it has to be true. Takes one to know one and all that.'

The pair shared a smile.

'So where are we going?' Asked Stacey, looking from side to side inquisitively.

'Well, I don't know about you, but I thought that we could maybe continue what we started earlier?'

Stacey felt a tingle, trying her best to hide her excitement.

'And what exactly was it that we started?'

'Well, if I recall,' Rufus grabbed Stacey gently by her shoulders. 'I had you against the toilet wall.' He then led her to the nearest building - The bakery opposite the tavern - and sidled into the alley beside it.

Stacey went with it, acting out the scene as if it were rehearsed. The alley was much less grimy than the ones she was used too.

'Then what?' She breathed coyly.

'Then, if memory serves, you pulled up your skirt.'

She obliged, lifting it slowly, watching his reaction as it rose.

'And then?' She asked.

Rufus caressed the back of her legs until his hands met the dip behind her knees. He lifted her, forcefully pressing her against the wall until her legs were straddling his hips. Stacey exhaled, squeaking a little with excitement, she followed the squeak with a purr as she wrapped her arms around Rufus' back and neck.

There was no place for romance anymore, this was carnal. Rufus fumbled around at his crotch with one hand, trying clumsily to unzip his jeans. Stacey ran her fingers across his hair as he buried his face into her cleavage, something he'd longed to do all night. He'd just about found his member when a sound shattered the moment. The passion had left as quickly as it had arrived when the pair heard the sound of someone's fist pummeling the Ashen Maid's front door. The pair straightened themselves out, making sure that their bits were covered.

'And then,' Muttered Rufus 'the Landlord showed up, and spoiled the fucking day!'

Rufus held his finger up to his lips and shushed, Stacey acknowledged him with a nod. He edged his way up the alley until he could spot where the commotion was coming from. He saw a man in a brightly coloured anorak hitting the tavern door, so hard that he was close to taking it off its hinges.

Eugene swung his fists with all that his stringy arms could muster. He felt his palms bruise, but he didn't care. He started yelling, demanding that the shady barman made himself known, all the while checking the clearing to the moor.

A light came on behind the glass and a disgruntled voice came from behind the wood.

'What is it? What on earth is worth breaking my bloody door over?'

The tavern owner opened the door a crack.

'What is it? What do you want?'

Eugene fell against the door, trying to push his way in. The tavern owner struggled to hold the door back.

'The man, the barman from earlier, the bastard that fed me drinks all night, where is he?'

'Look, I don't know you and we're closed. Back up now, don't make me tell you again!'

Eugene gave up pushing.

'I just want the man, the evil bastard that got me pissed and sent me out there!' He pointed towards the opening and the moors beyond it.

'I don't remember you.' The tavern owner shook his head. 'This is a small village and I know everyone here. If there's a new face at the bar, I'd recognise it.'

'No, it wasn't you, it was the other guy, the taller, thinner man.'

The tavern owner was lost, he contorted his face as he tried to make sense of the mad man's rants.

'You're mistaken friend. I work the bar…' He placed his hand on his chest. 'alone. If you got a drink here, it would have been from me.'

'No, you're lying!' Barked Eugene as he thundered into the door once more.

'That's it! I've had it.' Grunted the tavern owner as he used the last of his strength to push the door shut. 'I have a gun,' Came his muffled voice from behind the door. 'I *will* use it you understand? Now fuck off!'

Eugene was too enraged to care. As he raised his fist once more he felt it snag in midair. Rufus had crept over and grabbed his wrist. Eugene turned around, his eyes wide. His arm was jittering in Rufus' grip. He'd expected to see someone - or something - else standing behind him. When he noticed Rufus he became both relieved and confused.

'What are you doing?' Asked Rufus.

Eugene didn't respond.

'Look fella, I don't know what's going on, but you can't do this.'

'I need to speak someone, someone inside.'

Rufus let his wrist go. Eugene rubbed it with his other hand and shook his head, he was exhausted.

'It can wait till morning can't it?'

Stacey made her way out of the shadows, walking over to Rufus gingerly. Eugene watched her as she approached. The young couple seemed to bring him back to reality; usually he was reserved, quiet, and the sudden company made him aware of just how contrary he was acting.

'I suppose it can.' Said Eugene humbly.

Rufus placed his arm over Eugene's shoulder and begun to comfort him as best he could. Slowly they started heading away from the tavern and towards the lodge. Rufus was the be the good Samaritan tonight, whether he liked it or not.

Stacey lulled behind, her attention drawn to the clearing to the moors. She tried her hardest to pierce the darkness, her eyes slits and head tilted forward. Some light from the village illuminated the end of the path and it's dissipation of cobbles into mud and grass. Beyond that was an abyss, it was darker than dark. She wasn't sure why but her gaze was drawn into it like light to a black hole. She saw no shapes, heard no sounds, but she was convinced that the darkness was staring back at her. An urge took her and cautiously she begun to approach the moors. She'd taken two steps before Rufus noticed her. He called out her name, twice before she'd snapped out of her trance.

'Let's get back.' said Rufus.

Stacey nodded, double-checking the clearing as she caught up with the others. She hooked her arm through Rufus', his other arm was propping up Eugene. Stacey, with a shake of her head and a few vigorous blinks had forgotten. Disregarding any feelings she might have felt as being paranoia, a trick of the light (or lack of it). She focused now on the hard bicep in her grip, cursing the old man for ruining what could have been a wonderful night.

On a clear night you could maybe pick up a channel or two. All that Lawrence Mumford had to watch tonight was white noise with an occasional a blurred face. They would appear for a second, then fizzle out. The hissing sound would make his teeth grit, so he'd mute his television until a picture could establish itself. This wasn't happening tonight, no matter how often he'd slap the side of his television set and he would slap it till his hand was black.

Larry - as he was known in the village - couldn't sleep. Not since he'd been woken earlier in the night by a madman at his door. He had taken out his shotgun and propped it against his bedside cabinet. He never loaded it, he owned some shells, but kept them rooms away from the gun.

He sat up in bed and switched off the T.V., throwing his remote control onto the floor to alleviate his frustration. This happened a lot and he had learned to throw the remote with just the right amount of force, ensuring that it wouldn't break. It was an art form. Larry checked the clock and couldn't believe the time, he fell back into his mattress and rolled onto his side. Fluffing his pillows with his fists and then burying his head in it.

Larry the Landlord had bought the Ashen Maid seven years ago hoping to spend the rest of his days in a quiet village where everyone would know his name. He has lived above the bar alone for much too long. He'd always hoped for a wife but she never came along. Short, chubby old and balding, he didn't stand much of a chance. He portrayed himself as a bit of a tough guy for the punters - often parading about the bar with a shaved head and chest puffed out - but this was just a role he played. The illusion would be shattered the moment he'd open his mouth; As a teenager his voice never quite finished breaking. He was forever cursed with a croaky whine that most found irritating.

No matter how hard he pressed his lids together he couldn't will himself to sleep. Usually the sound of a violent gale and thunderous rainstorm against his window would relax him, remind him of just how cosy and safe he was in his bed. The storm of the century wouldn't send him to sleep tonight. The old man that was at his door earlier had rattled him, something he'd said that he couldn't shake from his mind.

A country pub - like the Ashen Maid - would need certain things to become a success; The quaint countryside décor that you would expect. Wholesome, farmed food washed down with a selection of local ales, and finally - and most importantly - a myth.

Tourists love nothing more than a haunted pub. Those that have the most interesting ghost stories seem to make the most money. People would travel from miles around just to sit at a bar and hope to catch a glimpse of the supernatural. These pubs are no different from any other, no better, no worse, but the hunger for proof is something many would pay through the teeth for. You could ask these visitors whether they'd seen a shadow at the corner of their eye or noticed a pint glass move and most would say no. This didn't matter, they had already arrived, paid more than they should have and left through the gift shop.

The Ashen Maid had tales of its own. Larry, in his seven years here was yet to see anything but the locals had passed on their experiences. Being a devout sceptic, Larry had dismissed them as drunken fantasies, but there was always a common denominator in the stories told to him. A tall, thin man that would lurk in the shadows behind the bar.

Tossing and turning in his bed, Larry had let the hiker's claims play on his mind. He couldn't understand why it bothered him so. If he were to feel a chill, it was because of a draft somewhere. If he heard a creak, it was the wooden beams and floorboards shrinking in the cold night. Larry could explain everything away, and comfort himself better than anyone else could.

It may have been the desperation in the man's face, the throbbing veins in his temples, but the man seemed convinced. Ready to kill whoever it was that sent him out into the moors. If it was an act it was Oscar-worthy, and if the man was mad, then Larry might've wished he'd kept a couple of buckshot shells a little closer to the gun.

He could hear the tavern door again, a banging too rhythmic to be the wind. Larry thought it might be his mind replaying the memory from earlier, his lack of sleep playing tricks with him. This was not the case, there was someone at the door, and whoever it was, was desperate to get in.

'That bastard, that fucking bastard!' Growled Larry as he got out of bed, grabbing the shotgun on the way out of the bedroom.

He stormed down the stairs in his vest and boxer shorts, gripping the gun with both hands. He wrung it as if it were a neck.

'I told you I had a gun!' He yelled as he entered the bar. 'I told you I would use it!'

Larry felt the foam in his mouth, it crept out at the corners. It always would when he'd get worked up like this.

The door continued to be beaten, the thumps were constant and louder than before. Larry held the shotgun up to the amber glass pane in the door, hoping to deter the man.

'You see this?' He tapped on the glass with the gun butt. 'This is my gun!'

He knew it wasn't loaded but that never mattered before. He'd cleared his share of unwanted from the bar in his time here, the sight of a gun - in England - was shock enough.

'If I open this door, it won't end well, you hear?'

For a moment his threat seemed to work. The banging had stopped. Larry held his ear closer to the door, hoping to hear footsteps moving away. Mere inches away from the wood and the door began to thunder again, more violently this time.

'That's it, bastard!' Screamed Larry as he swung open the door.

Waving the gun ahead of him, he moved it from side to side hoping to aim at the culprit. There was only an empty, rain-beaten street, lit eerily by a sporadic street lamps. There wasn't a soul in sight. Stepping into the street, unnerved but alert, he yelled 'Hello?' only to be answered by an ominous gust that blew in from the moors.

The gust was all the answer he needed; It wasn't possible for a person to knock on the door and get away so soon. The wind was strong, and despite his earlier dismissal, he had decided that it must have been the elements breaking his door down. As hypocritical as it was, this was satisfaction enough for him to turn around and get back into the warmth.

It was only a few steps to the door but he froze mid stride. The moors begged his attention, and what he saw awoke a terror in him; on the horizon - where the first light had begun to turn the night sky blue - he spotted a glow. A fire burning in the distance. It was only a spec but the sight of it made his knees weak. A deep-rooted, forgotten memory had been freed.

'It matters not, when the pyre's lit…' mumbled Larry, the words having a life of their own and spilling from his mouth unintentionally.

He hadn't a moment to lose. He leapt inside, slamming the door behind him. Beads of sweat forming on his brow even though he still felt the bitter chill from outside. Grasping his shotgun for dear life he suddenly remembered that is was empty. Cursing his pacifism, he tossed it to the ground and sprinted towards the stairwell. It was for only a moment, but he was sure that he'd seen someone behind the bar as he passed; a tall, thin, shadow of a man. There were bigger things to fear tonight if the legends were true.

Larry could think of nothing better to do than lock his bedroom door and cower behind it. This fear of his was irrational and unfounded but something was coming. He could feel it in his heart, his heart that seemed to choke as if it were in the clasp of icy talons.

Slowing his breath, he listened through the crack in the door and heard the creaking of floorboards. There was no dismissing it now, it wasn't the cold night shrinking the wood, it was the sound of something heading to his way. As it approached it brought a cloud of dust that rushed under his bedroom door to greet him. The invader waited outside, it's presence was wicked and it teased the hairs on Larry's arms to stand. He felt a tear freeze to his cheek as his breath become fog.

'*It matters not, when the pyre's lit…*' Came a whisper, ethereal and sinister behind the wood so close to Larry's ear. '*…if you run, or hide, or stand, or sit.*'.

Larry begun to mouth the words, as if they were his last.

'*A bitter wind, pass plain and clod…*'

The windows begun to shudder as the rain and wind tried desperately to get inside.

'*…You're on your own… no hope… no God!*'

The final word of the verse was its cue. The windows swung open, and those that couldn't swing free shattered. Lawrence Mumford's screams went unheard, masked by the maelstrom that had found its way into the Ashen Maid that night.

2

No storm lasts forever. This morning the sun had a chance to shine. It found its way through the curtains and decided to lay across Finn's brow. He winced, the light piercing his brain, every beam a slice. He wasn't allowed to rest, the heavens wouldn't allow it, and the sun only shone because he wished it not to. A hangover is never a pleasant experience for anyone, but for Finn it was torture. The room was too warm, the light too bright, the pain too much. He had a knack for self-pity, a habit of his that was not infectious, no matter how much he'd sought sympathy.

As he rolled over with a groan he noticed an empty bed; Rufus was not there. The bed was made and it begged the question; what time *is* it? 10:35 according to the clock on the wall. Breakfast finishes at eleven and he was damned if he was going to miss a free meal.

Throwing on last night's clothes he stopped by the bathroom to splash his face. He'd read that the water was hard here but this was ridiculous; the water was the colour of weak tea, and nowhere near as warm.

The breakfast room was cluttered. A few doily covered tables surrounded by musty ornaments. It could have been a fully stocked antiques shop if the owner could ever part with anything. Judging by this room, she never had. Stuffed animals stood in ferocious poses along the sideboards, animals no more intimidating than ferrets, or hares. Deer heads of all sizes where mounted along the wall, arranged with no rhyme or reason.

As mismatched as the decorations and ornaments were, there was a running theme that connected them all; a thick layer of dust. The air was foggy with it, and as Rufus sat down to order some breakfast, he knew that Finn wasn't going to be happy entering this room, let alone eating in it.

Rufus, Stacey and Jessica were the only guests seated for breakfast. They chose a table in the centre of the room - at Stacey's request - to keep their distance from any of the animal corpses, their beady eyes that seemed to watch her wherever she went. Lined up and perched, ready to snatch the food from their plates.

They had been waiting a while, chatting and having the occasional laugh about the night's events. Even Jessica managed a smile or two. The lodge keeper was yet to be seen, but the clattering of plates and the bubble of boiling water could be heard beyond a beaded curtain that obscured the kitchen. As polite as Rufus was, there was a limit to his patience.

'Service!' He called. 'Could murder a cup of coffee!'

He was ignored it seemed as the commotion in the kitchen continued, unperturbed.

Finn had made it downstairs, stopping as he reached the breakfast room's threshold. He squinted through aching eyes, scanning the room and shaking his head, appalled by the filth and afraid of the dust cloud that would torture his lungs.

'I knew this would happen.' Said Rufus.

'The state of this place!' Groaned Finn.

'I know, I know. All I ask is that you try.'

Finn took a few steps in, hesitantly approaching their table.

'It's disgusting,' He said. 'I can't believe we're gonna eat here!?'

'I agree, I really do. But after last night, I could eat a horse.'

'Have a look around here,' She examined the walls. 'I'm sure we can find you one.' Joked Jessica.

The table sniggered. Suddenly Finn was reminded of his performance last night, and a cramping anxiety took grip of his innards. He didn't want to face Jessica, he could have sworn he loved her last night, an exaggeration of course. He had declared such feelings before, and with much less to drink.

'Morning Finn, how are you feeling today?' Asked Jessica, wryly.

She had decided to lay off him, taking note of her friends advice last night while she laid awake in bed, alone.

'I'm fine Jessica, thanks for asking.' He answered, officially.

He sat down, sweeping the dust away from the space on the table in front of him. The other three continued their earlier conversation while Finn put on a brave face, forcing a smile when he felt a joke was being told. His head still pounded and his joints still ached but he was no longer after sympathy, instead he hoped to build bridges. For this to happen, he would have to be normal, taking a leaf out of Rufus' book, even mirroring him from time to time. An act that didn't go unnoticed by his best friend who knew him so well.

The bead curtain was disturbed as the old woman - who smelt of old seashells - made herself known. She dragged her heels across the floorboards, brandishing a notepad and pencil. She was thin and gaunt, but her silvery hair had volume. Preened and plumped earlier that morning. She wore makeup, blatantly so, bold blues and reds filling the cracks around her eyes and mouth. She may have been a beauty once, never accepting the decay of time. Now she resembled a drag queen, one that would never make it to the main stage.

'Gentleman, Ladies.' She coughed. 'What would you like?'

She stood, shakily by their table.

'Do you have a menu?' Asked Stacey.

'No menus, tell me what you want and I'll see to it.'

'I don't know about you lot, but I need coffee before I can even think about food.' Said Rufus.

'No coffee, only tea.'

'I suppose that will have to do then.'

'The rest of you want tea?'

They each nodded, mumbling please and thank you.

'Well alright, It's a start I guess.' Said the old lady, leaving the group and heading back into the kitchen.

'Delightful.' Breathed Stacey, rolling her eyes.

He was hungry but had no interest in eating this morning. Eugene was up and away as soon as he was able, taking to the streets on a mission that a night's sleep did little to perturb. What alcohol poisoned him last night was gone and still a rage stoke up hot coals in his chest. He had questions, and a tall, thin, shadow of a man was going to answer them.

The Ashen Maid was still. Among the bustle of a waking village the tavern seemed to be at rest. Eugene passed (and ignored) a few villagers along his journey who made an effort to say good morning, some a little wounded by the old man's indifference. He was blinkered as he approached the tavern door, his momentum failing to cease as he hit his head on the beam across the eave, the same beam that he had been so careful to avoid before. He rubbed his head and sucked in some air through his teeth. This gave him a moment to notice the door, and the fact that it was open a crack. He gave it a delicate prod to be sure, and sure enough it opened.

'Hello?' Yelled Eugene as he took a step in.

There was no reply. The bar was empty, neat and undisturbed, ready for the lunchtime rush. Eugene moved to the corner where he'd been manipulated, hoping to catch the mysterious bartender polishing a glass. No such luck. Just being there added fuel to his fire, the scene took him back to the night. He remembered just how helpless he was, how easily he was seduced. It was shameful, and the fact that the stranger had used his beloved Ethel to do this was unforgivable.

He made his way upstairs, searching each room with a quick glance and repeatedly shouting; 'Show yourself, Bastard!'. It was clear that the tavern was empty, if there had been a soul there Eugene would have felt it. Eugene entered Lawrence's bedroom and noticed the unmade bed. It suddenly dawned on him that he was in someone's home.

Collecting himself he examined the room a little closer. The floor at his feet had been marked, three or four scratches leading out of the bedroom and along the floorboards. The marks were in a row, spaced out as if they were made by fingernails, occasionally ending and starting again as he followed the trail down the stairwell. The wood was dense, the varnish tough, yet the marks were fresh. Eugene considered this and wondered how someone could manage it? He imagined the pain of his own fingers scratching at the wood, the splinters under his nails, it made him wince.

He followed the trail apprehensively which led him back to the bar. It continued under the counter flap then ended at a large decorative rug, at the ominous end of the bar. The marks continued underneath, Eugene kicked at it with his feet until a corner of the rug folded over. He noticed a seam in the floorboards, as he pulled the rest of the rug away he revealed what seemed to be a trapdoor. His old eyes didn't work as well as they used to, he had to kneel, hesitantly. The claw marks ended at the seam that whistled with air. Whoever had struggled so, had ended up here.

Eugene had lost his spectacles on the moors, he had to narrow his eyes to notice the crude etching on the trap door. It read; *Lawrence Mumford, murdered on this spot, 2013*. The words had been scratched into the wood, looking like a child's first written words. It reminded him of the brass plaques he'd seen along the street, and like the others he'd seen, the name meant nothing to him.

It unnerved him, the fact that it was hidden like this. It made it feel personal, a trail for only him to follow. He felt that he had been lured there and though each fibre of his being wanted to stand up and leave, he found his hand clasping the brass loop attached to the trapdoor. He tugged, letting dust, and a vacuum of air free. He waved his hand, tried to clear the cloud and then noticed the black below. The hole seemed deep and malevolent. It wheezed like a cancerous gullet. Eugene's curiosity had had more than it's fill, he wished to see no more. He stood up, suddenly feeling a presence behind him, turning on a penny to confront it. The man; the tall, thin shadow of a man greeted him with a smile, mere inches from his face. The man's eyes were hollow, black as the pit at his feet. Eugene blurted the word, 'You!' before feeling an icy finger prod his chest.

It sent him back a step, a step more than the floorboards could accommodate and he fell. Hitting his head on the way down he tumbled into the darkness unconscious, not knowing if he would wake up a shattered mess or fall forever more, obliviously.

The tea wasn't half bad, but whether it was worth the wait was debatable. Lucille Tourney had run the lodge for years, served more breakfasts than she could count, but each breakfast seemed to slow her pace, practice proving far from perfect. She lost a little drive each and every morning, a little bit of her soul was served up with each English breakfast. Yet she played the part as best she could, would even try to smile now and then. She didn't appreciate how her face would resemble a walnut when she did. So many lines, so little to show for them.

The cutlery chinked as she lay two breakfasts down sloppily. After a lengthy shuffle back to the kitchen, she returned with two more. Each plate at first glance was the same; a traditional English breakfast with all the trimmings. On closer inspection there were subtle differences; a missing sausage, an extra rasher of bacon. The measurements were slapdash and unfair and it was clear that Lucille didn't care. Breakfast was served, that was enough for her. Her job was done.

Finn noticed movement at the corner of his eye. A black spec dancing around their table, deciding to land by his food. It was a housefly to most but not to Finn. To him it was pestilence, it was filth and it was enough to turn him off his food. He slapped his hand down, popping the insect under his palm and leaving a smear on the tablecloth. Lucille watched and offered Finn a look of contempt. It wasn't just the stain he'd made, it seemed to be something more, as if the bug was a pet of hers that Finn had just murdered.

She moved closer to the table and leaned in, the guests watched in anticipation.

'You ever feel an itch?' She asked. 'A tingle on your skin and you can't understand why?'

Finn shrugged his shoulders, wiping his hand with a napkin and offering Lucille a blank look.

'You scratch your arm, swearing blindly that there was something running around on it, but there's nothing to see?'

'I guess.' Mumbled Finn.

'You know what that is?' Lucille directed the question to the whole table.

They each offered a look similar to Finn's.

'It's every bug you kill, every fly you swat or spider you tread on.' She said.

Rufus begun to chuckle, stopping immediately when he realised it wasn't a joke.

'Every creature you kill, no matter how small, how insignificant *you* may think they are, *will* haunt you.' Whispered Lucille intensely.

'Ah, come on,' Blurted Stacey. 'You don't really believe that do you?'

Lucille didn't reply, she just looked at Stacey and exhaled in defeat.

'Hold on a minute lady, it's like a… A petting zoo graveyard in here.' Explained Finn, presenting the room to her with a wave of his arms, as if she didn't know each and every animal in the room by name.

'I didn't kill them. I rescued them.' She protested.

'Well I'd say you were a little late, wouldn't you?' He jested, coaxing a laugh from the table.

Lucille shook her head, hoping to kill Finn with a vicious glare. When she couldn't manage it she turned away and headed into the kitchen, cursing the children under her breath as she went.

'What the hell was that?' Asked Rufus as the coast became clear.

'Village folk quirks, I guess.' Said Jessica.

'I wouldn't say quirky. Insane, maybe.'

Finn batted a few beans around his plate with a knife. Rufus tucked into his food, shoveling it down with barely a chew, Finn watched in envy. He was torn; The echo of his empty stomach cried out for food but his neuroses wouldn't allow a thing past his lips, not in this place. The crazy lady could have done anything to his plate in the privacy of her kitchen. It made him shudder, the thought of her even touching it, as if crazy was infectious. He dropped his knife with a clank.

'Nope, not doing it!' He blurted.

'What's wrong, buddy?' Asked Rufus.

'I can't do it, I'm not eating this.'

'Really?' He mumbled with his mouth full. 'It's pretty good.'

Stacey and Jessica nodded, agreeing with an approving 'yum.'.

'You don't know what's behind that beaded curtain, that kook. I bet she strokes these animals every morning, her pets, calling out to them by name, names like Poppet and Twinkle… And I *bet* she forgets to wash her hands, stirring the baked beans with her fingers.'

The girls stopped chewing, their faces dropping.

'Don't do this Finn, just 'cos you can't eat it, don't ruin it for the rest of us.'

Finn remembered his promise to himself, to be normal this morning.

'Don't mind me, forget I said anything. Enjoy your meals.'

Jessica dropped her hands, resting her cutlery on the table.

'I don't think I can, now!' She said, staring at Finn. 'So what do you suggest? We need to eat.'

'Speak for yourself.' Interrupted Stacey.

'Well, I'm gonna find a café, or a shop or something.' Said Finn.

'Sounds like a plan,' Jessica stood up. 'Let's go.'

Finn never expected her boldness, her sudden assertion. It was not the girl he'd met last night. Jessica had taken on a roll this morning, she was to be someone much more confident than herself. All Finn could do was nod as he slid his chair under the table, Jessica was already on her way out of the room.

'You two go, have fun, I'll catch up with you later.' Said Rufus, still chomping his breakfast.

Stacey saw this as an opportunity, taking advantage of her friends unexpected absence and using it to spend a little quality time with her potential mate. Quality time that had been stolen from her last night.

It was a nice day. The cacophony of wind and rain the night before seemed to have cleared the way for a blue sky. It was even a little warm when out of the shade. All that remained of the storm last night was the blinding glisten of puddles that collected in the poorly designed streets. Golgothaan wasn't big, Finn and Jessica had managed a lap of the village in under fifteen minutes, and this was at a slow, leisurely pace. As for getting something to eat, all they could find was a small bakery that had been frozen in time. You could imagine customers queuing, desperate with ration books in hand.

The bread and cakes were freshly made, this was clear. The heart-warming smell was testament to this. Finn had no issues with eating anything here, he enjoyed a Belgium bun, his favourite. Jessica argued that it was too early for sweets but Finn protested with a gleeful chomp, followed by a satisfied smile.

The Ashen maid was across the road, it sat silently while the rest of the village seemed to thrive. Catching sight of the tavern made Finn cringe, he felt shameful just to linger outside so he urged that they move on, surprisingly Jessica obeyed. They made their way back past the Scarlett Inn and Jessica pointed out a spire beyond the roofs. It was a black cross, elaborate and ornate and Jessica wished to investigate further, after all this was not just a holiday for her.

It was a building out of place and time. The Church stood among the buildings like a peacock among pigeons. It was twice as tall as anything else in Golgothaan and seemed to be much older. It had a style that Jessica failed to place; light grey stone with black marble, embellished with stone figures, carved directly into the walls. These figures were in poses and scenarios that were unfamiliar to Jessica, who prided herself on her biblical knowledge. A particular scene, etched above the front doors, was most impressive.

'Beautiful, isn't it.' She said, marveling at the building.

'It's certainly something.' Replied Finn, feigning interest to gain favour.

They stood opposite the huge, black front doors, of which one was ajar enough to allow visitors inside.

'What is a building like this doing here?' She wondered.

Finn cocked his head to one side, hoping to tease a legitimate opinion from it.

'Perhaps this church was here first, the village might have grown up around it.'

'I don't doubt that, but the look of it, I can't place it. Can't place the century.'

'I wouldn't have a clue, I won't even try to guess.' Said Finn as he watched Jessica raise her head to the spire. 'You wanna go in?'

Jessica turned to Finn and gave him a smile, she hooked her arm through his.

'I'd like that, very much.'

She'd taken him by surprise, the warmth of her against his forearm, all he could do was offer a shaky nod and an unattractive smile. She led him in nonetheless.

The black marble underfoot lent a tap to each of their steps, the sound amplified by the church's design. The outside of the church paled to the interior, even Finn was impressed. Murals covered the ceiling, paintings to rival the Sistine chapel. As she looked around all she could think was; *this is a waste.* Architecture like this belonged in a city, where countless tourists could visit and be in awe, just as she was. It was a shame to hide it away like this, Golgothaan didn't deserve it.

They were not alone, several parishioners were planted on pews, some stoic, while others conversed as quietly as they could. An elderly woman was at the front, chatting with a priest. He must have been funny, because woman seemed to laugh with everything she had. Perhaps he was flirting with her Jessica thought, their body language would suggest so, and for an older man, he had maintained his looks.

Finn and Jessica walked down the centre aisle, still arm in arm.

'It's like we're getting married.' She jested.

Her joke made him a little uncomfortable, Finn, ever uptight, assuming that this was a proposal of sorts.

'H-Ha, yeah,' He squirmed. 'but if this was a wedding, then I'd be giving you away.'

'Ah yes, I suppose you would be. I wonder, whose waiting for me at the end of the aisle? I hope he's hot.' She laughed.

He hadn't expected to feel even more insecure. He hid it with a joke.

'Well, he didn't ask for my blessing anyhow!'

'Traditionalist are ya?'

'In a church like this, how could you not be?'

Jessica smiled, knowing just how uncomfortable she'd made him, judging every one of his responses in an attempt to know Finn just that little bit better. She could read people, and once upon a time toyed with the subject of psychology rather than history, though her heart would never have been in it. She ushered Finn to a pew, where they both sat in contemplative silence.

If he was dead, his hip wouldn't ache like this. He couldn't be sure if he'd opened his eyes or not, it was pitch black either way. Where the hell was he? The ground under him was soft and slick, as he gripped it, it squeezed through his fingers. It was mud, he was sure of it, the texture was like clay, just like the ground beneath Golgothaan. This he knew, stuff like this interested him. The fact that is was damp was probably due to the poor drainage in the village, and the torrential downpour from the night before.

As he wheezed and groaned he gauged the size of the hole he lay in. His voice was deadened, suggesting to him that the walls were very close. It was time to get up, which was somewhat of a task at his age when he wasn't falling through trapdoors. He flipped onto his hands and knees, sliding around in the mud, then stood, hands held out above his head to check for a ceiling. His bones clicked and creaked, the pain was almost too much, he couldn't help but sob a little. Pride meant nothing here.

Eugene was not nearly as afraid as he felt he should have been. Maybe it was the gratitude of surviving the fall, though he wasn't one hundred percent sure if he had. Since Ethel's passing, he'd often long for death, though a religious childhood had instilled the fear of hell in him. Suicide was a direct route there, to a place where Ethel was surely not, so he'd taken to the attitude that he had nothing left to lose.

There was mud above his head, that he traced with his fingers until he reached the walls, mapping out the layout in his mind. It sloped steeply upwards behind him, most likely where he'd fallen and slid to break his fall, he could see no crack of light from the trapdoor above it. A slight breeze came from ahead that seemed to beckon him towards it. It seemed fresh, though any new air would in the stagnancy of the cavern.

Moving forward, he held one hand in front while the other traced the wall to his left. He'd read somewhere that if you were ever lost in a maze, keep one hand on the left wall and you'd be sure to find your way out. This rule was likely to be of no use, but he praised himself for thinking of it anyway. His fingers dragged a line in the mud until they would hit rocks. There were more and more rocks the further in he went, breaking his stride, the feel of the slop between his fingers had become quite satisfying.

The dark was disorientating, he felt like he'd walked a mile, but it was most likely much, much less. He'd felt something among the rocks and mud, a cord of some sort. Gripping it tightly, he followed it until he reached what felt like a metal box. It was a relief to feel something manmade, a little slice of modernity in the primordial blackness. Fumbling in the dark, he examined it, his feelers discovering a rod of some kind. It was a lever, that he pulled without hesitation. It was damp - like everything else - and sparks burst from it as electricity found its way into the darkness. A row of crudely hung lights came to life, blinding Eugene, hiding his eyes behind his hands until he could regain focus. The loneliness was now subdued, the mystery removed as a simple mud tunnel was revealed to him in an amber glow. It branched off in several directions, and behind him were routes that he had missed on the right.

The walls, that had seemed peppered with rocks were not peppered with rocks at all. Eugene noticed the grey matt of the objects, and as he pulled one free he noticed the hollow that his finger had gripped was an eye socket. The rocks, every one of them, were skulls.

He dropped it as soon as he'd realised, recoiling in disgust. Suddenly the mystery was back, more sinister than before. Despite the pain in his hip he moved with determination, hoping to find a way out. Turning left and right, desperate to escape the hundreds of hollow eyes that watched his every move.

It had taken time, but the peaceful setting - that was in its own way romantic - had allowed the couple open up. Finn had begun to find his feet with Jessica, and had at last become himself. They had chatted for an hour, the mellow organ music - that was played on a hidden speaker somewhere - had a comforting effect, and it was the perfect soundtrack to their newfound connection.

Even Jessica had dropped her defenses, something which she would rarely do. Insecure in her own way, her bravado was a cover, and as her confidence grew she would dislike herself that little bit more. It was a breath of fresh air to sit and converse and get past Finn's neuroses, finding a man that she could see herself - after a lot more work - possibly falling for.

The priest had done his rounds, mingling among the parishioners like a celebrity, gracing them with his presence. Finn and Jessica, who sat away from the others, were the only two he'd not spoken with today. He turned his attention to the new faces. He knew that he was interrupting them, but this was his house.

'Welcome, friends. How are we today?' He asked, his voice like velvet.

The pair resented the interruption, but were too polite to show it.

'Good afternoon, Father.' Said Jessica. Phony smile and all.

'I don't think we've met.'

'No, we haven't. My friend and I are just visiting.'

'Tourists? Golgothaan doesn't get many of those,' He smiled. 'it is always nice to welcome new, young faces to *Our Lady on the Moors*.'

Finn nodded, grinning at some effort. Jessica looked at him and then did the same, but her smile came much more naturally.

'It is a beautiful church,' Said Jessica. 'a true diamond in the rough.'

The priest looked around, like he didn't already know every inch of the place.

'It truly is a blessed place, its beauty never fails to move me.'

'You must be very proud.'

'As far as parishes go, I could have done much, much worse.'

He held out his hand, inviting Jessica to take it, his eyes rarely directed at Finn.

'Father Thomas Hogan,' He shook her hand. 'and you are?'

'Jessica.' She said, quickly slipping from his grip.

Finn shook it also, though Father Thomas had taken his hand back before he could say his name.

'So are you married or just living in sin?' He joked, laughing softly.

'Us?' Blurted Jessica. 'We're just friends. We met yesterday.'

It was the only reply Jessica could be expected to make, but it hurt Finn nonetheless.

'Really, is that so?' Said Father Thomas, his eyes suddenly acquiring a slight twinkle.

The priest's body language had changed, the smile he wore had become slimier. Father Thomas Hogan was relatively young to be a priest, though his side-parted hair had a few strands of grey, his body becoming the stereotype one would expect to see behind a pulpit. He was handsome, in a clean cut kind of way, and Jessica hadn't failed to notice this. But being a devout atheist, the man seemed as ridiculous to her as his beliefs did.

Jessica was aware of Finn's discomfort. The pair of them were on to Thomas, who given more time would have edged closer and closer, inching across the pew until his warmth would become intimate with hers.

'Well, Father Hogan, it's been an absolute pleasure,' She stood up. 'but me and my *new* friend must be on our way.'

Finn stood up also, following Jessica like a child following its mother, never quite sure of where she was going, but following her loyally nonetheless. Father Thomas was a little wounded as he slipped out of the pew, almost forced out by the leaving couple. He stood, still trying to smile as they made their way to the exit.

'Pleasure to meet you both.' He called out as they left his sight.

'If that guy was a cartoon wolf, his tongue would have unraveled to the floor and his eyes would have been on stalks!' Jested Finn as they made their way down the street.

Jessica laughed.

'Oh I don't know about that,' She said modestly, 'but he was somewhat of a slime ball.'

'For a man of the cloth, certainly.'

He was glad that she agreed, and now as they headed back towards the Scarlet Lodge, he was grateful for the morning they'd shared, her brashness at breakfast that had led to the foundations they had built. As negative as he usually was, even he could see the start of something here, and despite Jessica's defences, he could tell that she was just as interested as he was.

She couldn't roll, so much as peel herself away from Rufus' chest. The lovers were naked, slick with sweat, and panting after a particularly exhausting session. The air was thick, the windows foggy and the room seemed saturated by their acts. The Scarlet Lodge hadn't seen this much action in years, and it felt sacrilegious almost to be in such a setting; the building so quaint and innocent. It didn't stop them though, not once, nor twice.

'You know, usually, a guy that looks like you, is as cocky as you are, they don't follow through. They talk a good game but when it comes to the crunch... Big disappointment.' Stacey stretched her arms above her head, squirming under the sheets contently. 'But you, big fella, you're the whole package ain't ya.'

'Well, you wouldn't be the first to say so.' Said Rufus, smugly.

'Been around the block have we?'

'Don't pretend *you* haven't.'

'Me? I'm a good girl.'

'You're anything but, some of your moves... You taught me a thing or two today.'

Stacey rolled towards Rufus, laying her arm across his chest, her head resting on his shoulder.

'*She's a creative girl*, my teachers would often say, but then I did have that thing with Mr. Quinn.'

'Art teacher?'

'Nope, geography if you can believe it.'

Rufus chuckled. Stacey watched his reaction, disappointed that he seemed completely indifferent to her sexual past. She hoped to spot a little jealousy, to gauge his feelings towards her. Emotionally immature, this was the only way she knew how. It was difficult for a girl like Stacey. Getting a guy was easy, keeping them proved near impossible. The more guys she'd meet, the less guys would want to stay with her, it was a vicious cycle.

'What about you? Any stories to tell?' She asked.

'Like what?'

'I dunno, sex stories... Funny ones, exciting ones... Anything!'

Rufus continued to stare at the ceiling.

'I don't like to kiss and tell.'

'Ah come on, don't be a cliché. You've had your way with me, now you wanna lay there in silence.'

'It's my private life, same as this, and don't act like you didn't know what this was.'

Stacey moved back to her side of the bed.

'What do you mean?' She tried to hide the bitterness in her voice.

'I mean, this is a holiday, we had sex. This is what happens. Don't pretend that we'll be swapping numbers and calling each other the moment we get back to our real lives.'

Even Rufus knew that he'd crossed the line, he turned his head to see Stacey watery-eyed. She smiled as she climbed out of bed.

'You know, you're right.' She said, as she searched the floor for her clothes.

She stood facing the window, suddenly finding her modesty as she scrambled to get dressed. Rufus watched her, the light catching her curves, highlighting her breasts as they jiggled in the sun. As he watched he regretted his comment immediately, admiring her perfect body just reminded him that the chances of holding it again, had fallen dramatically.

'You don't have to go.' He said, halfheartedly.

'Hey, it's been fun,' She slipped on her shoes, 'I hope you and your creepy boyfriend enjoy the rest of your holiday.' She left the room, refusing to meet Rufus' eyes as she did so.

She was no sooner out of sight than out of mind. Rufus knew just how shallow he was, and strangely took reverence in it. He understood what life was; a series of encounters and experiences, some good, some bad. He took what he could, when he could, and would move on to the next thing that presented itself. There was no heaven or hell, no reward or punishment, and despite the occasional guilt he would feel for others, it would never deter him. Happiness was there to be had and he was going to have it while there was still life left to be lived.

Finn was the only person he'd let in, allowing himself to be closer to him than anyone else, even his own family, which was small and untypically cold. They were childhood friends, and remained that way through school and college, but even now, when he got down to the bones of it, he believed that if faced with an ultimatum, realistically his happiness was paramount.

Stacey's voice could be heard in the hall, complaints most likely to her friend and Finn that had returned from their morning walk. He sat up, prepared for his friend who entered their room.

'What did you do?' Growled Finn as he walked over to the Casanova.

'What?'

'You know what, we just met Stacey in the hall, yet another sobbing girl leaving the room of Rufus Granville.'

Finn stood over the bed, eyes wide.

'I don't know what's wrong with her, she was fine when she was sitting on my cock!'

'Charming!'

'Look what's the problem? We're on holiday, the girl was close to proposing.'

'I highly doubt it stud muffin, and my problem, believe it or not, is that if Stacey hates your guts, it don't bode well for me and Jessica.'

Rufus sat on the edge of the bed, his crotch barely covered by the sheet, watching Finn as he dropped into the armchair.

'So it went well?'

'Very well... very well for me, anyway.'

Rufus smiled.

'Good for you, buddy.'

'Well it doesn't matter now does it. You've fucked it *all* up!'

'Look, Finn, if it went as well as you say, Jessica's probably next door talking it over with Stacey. She'll talk her round, if this morning meant anything to her.'

Suddenly Finn was full of doubt. His neurosis had been hidden away all day. It found an opportunity to rear its ugly head.

'That's just it Rufus, it may come down to a morning spent with me, or a lifetime with her best friend.' He huffed. 'I don't stand a chance.'

Rufus stood up, moved to Finn and placed his giant, clammy hand on his shoulder.

'You don't give yourself enough credit, mate.'

Finn's eye line was drawn to Rufus' groin, mere inches from his face.

'Rufus!' Finn tried not to stare. 'Put some clothes on.'

An afternoon had passed. The sun began to die and in its place came dark clouds and the hum of a gale gathering strength. Finn had spent the time with a glass pressed to the wall, his ear now red and throbbing. He couldn't hear much, just a few words here and there.

His name was mentioned, but primarily Rufus was the subject of the day.

The voices had died about half an hour ago and Finn had finally decided to give up, his legs aching after hours of standing rigidly. Rufus was watching a small portable television, the picture degrading as the clouds moved in.

'Can I turn this up now?' He asked.

Finn slumped back into the armchair.

'Do what you want, I don't care.'

Rufus turned the volume up, but the static was almost unbearable.

'Piece of shit!' Mumbled Rufus as he tossed the remote to one side.

Through the intermittent hiss Finn heard a gentle rap on the door. He wasted no time in answering it. Taking a breath, he opened the door, casually, relieved to see Jessica's face.

'Jessic...' He said, but was cut short by Jessica shushing him with her finger pressed to her lips.

'She's asleep,' She whispered, 'do you fancy a drink, with me?'

Finn's face lit up.

'Absolutely.' He blurted, already closing the door behind him.

Rufus watched his friend leave without warning and muttered the word 'Nice.' resentfully.

The Ashen Maid was dead, doors locked and lights off. A few regulars hovered aimlessly outside, mumbling to each other. Some mumbled to themselves but all were equally lost without their evening tipple. They seemed hesitant to acknowledge the tourists, but Jessica made it impossible to be ignored.

'Excuse me, sir. Do you know why the pub is closed?'

An elderly man, sporting huge grey mutton chops, nervously held eye contact with her, though his eyes shook from left to right as he searched for another villager to come and save him.

'Sir, can you hear me?'

'I can 'ear you, Girl.' He snapped, his voice like sand paper. 'I don't know why the damned pub's closed.'

'Is it normally open?'

'Course it is, it's a bloody pub 'int it?'

Jessica's tolerance wore thin.

'I *mean*, could there be a reason it's closed? Do you know the Landlord?'

'Larry, that's 'is name, Larry the Landlord, see it's easy to remember. It rhymes.'

Jessica narrowed her eyes and shook her head.

'It doesn't rhyme... Look forget it.' Jessica feigned a smile. 'Thank you, you have been very helpful.'

She returned to Finn, hearing the elderly man grumble as she left.

'We won't be drinking here tonight.'

She turned to look at the moor at the end of the street. The half light created beautiful blue shapes on the horizon. The clouds that approached cast most of the sky in dark, while a slither of daylight seemed to struggle under the weight of it.

'Let's go out to the moors. Grab a bottle of something, from somewhere and spend some time together out there. I bet it's peaceful at night.'

Finn nodded emphatically, though he would have agreed to a night in a septic tank if she would join him.

The window needed fixing, it whistled with only the slightest breeze. Lucille had left her room till last, ensuring that the other rooms in the lodge were made habitable before her own. Money had dried up long ago, long before she could fix the draft.

She had grown attached to its tune, often laying in bed and listening to it, imagining that the faulty window was talking to her. She would ask it a question, and as a gust picked up the change in pitch and volume was a language that only she could understand. There were nights when it would tell a joke, and they would both laugh, their chortles both equally hearty and shrill.

Golgothaan was often plagued with wind, being on the moors there was no cover between the sea and the village. This meant that Lucille's companion was constant, and although the winters were bitter, she would make do with extra sheets rather than silencing her friend.

It was getting late and a few drops of rain had hit her bedroom window, the promise of another downpour to come. As she lay, her Bible in hand, she settled for the night, speaking out loud about her day and the ungrateful brats that she'd served breakfast to this morning. The window, as per usual, seemed to whistle at just the right moments. This, at the beginning of this bizarre relationship, convinced her that it was more than just some warped wood and glass.

'First customers in months, can you believe it?' She said.

'Woooo...' Came the draft.

'I know... I can't quite put my finger on it, but there's something wrong with that lot. Their souls are sour.'

Weeeee-ooooo...'

'You think so too?' Lucille rested the Bible on her chest. 'Back in the day I would have turned them away just as soon as they'd darkened our door. But, these things are sent to try us aren't they... And things are very, *very* tight.'

'Wooooo-eeeee-oooo...' The window raised its voice.

'I'm sorry?'

The rain picked up, the occasional patter became a barrage. The gale outside caused the draft to howl. Lucille seemed shocked by it.

'There's no need for that!' She snapped.

The wind continued, the howl becoming a roar that grew louder and more aggressive.

'Why are you being like this?' She stood up and threw on her dressing gown. 'I can't understand you, lower your voice.'

It refused as it filled the room with icy air and a deafening shriek. Lucille backed up to the bedroom door, afraid.

'I don't like this...' She tried to establish dominance by lowering her voice. 'I'm going to make myself a cup of tea, and when I get back... Well let's just say, I don't like this. Not one bit!'

She left the room, slamming the door behind her, resting against it for a moment as she composed herself. The warmth of the hallway comforted her as it usually would, reminding her of just how cold her bedroom was. She could still hear the window moan at her as she walked away, feeling like a disgruntled wife.

The kettle didn't howl, it whistled, reliably so. Lucille had an electric kettle but refused to use it. She thought it made the water taste different, artificial somehow, not like the traditional stovetop.

The ritual of making a cup of tea calmed her down, more than the drink itself.

Taking a sip, she caught her faded reflection in the kitchen window, outside being pitch black. For a moment she could see her younger self, the makeshift mirror blurring her lines, hiding her blemishes. She stroked her face and sighed. Her reminiscing was cut short by a rustle of the beaded curtain. It was a passing gust that left the beads swinging slightly, but it demanded her attention, knowing that the breakfast room windows were closed made her suspicious. She put down her tea and parted the beads, checking the breakfast room for the source of the breeze. The windows appeared sealed, but she made her way past the tables and stuffed animals to make sure anyway.

She ran her hand along the window rim, checking the bolts and hinges, and then moved away satisfied that it was locked tight. As she turned she felt another gust, one that brushed her neck intimately, making her body taught, her stomach cramped. Lucille felt eyes on her, not one of the dozens of glass marbles that her furry friends now had, but real, chilling, eyes. She scanned the room.

'Hello?' She whispered, dreading a reply.

It was silent, just long enough for her to take a breath, when suddenly the bay windows swung open with a force that sent her forward onto the floor. The curtains billowed as rain rushed in, drenching Lucille and half of the breakfast room. The sound of the storm drowned out her yelp as she lay, arm in front of her face to shield it from the torrent. It took all of her strength to make it to her feet. She moved slowly, fighting her way to the window, finally slamming it shut and cutting the dissonance short.

It took all she had to slow her heart, clutching at her chest as she slid the last latch into place, slapping it with her hand to ensure that it was fixed tight. Though the silence had returned, the hairs on the back of her neck remained up. She moved away from the window, hoping to rationalize it all. All she needed was a moment, a moment to catch her breath and think straight.

Lucille knew what it was like to feel alone, it was something that she couldn't explain yet knew better than anything else. She wasn't alone now, this she was sure of. Something had made its way into her home, and though she couldn't see it, she could feel its malevolence.

'What do you want?' She asked.

The room seemed to breath.

'Why are you here?' She turned on a penny. 'What do you want with me?'

Something moved, she caught sight of it in the corner of her eye. This room was her passion, the animals that she'd rescued, she knew each and every hair, tooth and claw. Arthur, the otter was missing, but strangely his wooden base remained. She approached it, flabbergasted, her hand held against her mouth. A voice broke her stride, little more than a whisper.

'It matters not...'

Lucille couldn't place the sound, but begun to doubt her collection as she checked each of them, ensuring that they were still mounted, still lifeless.

'When the pyre's lit...' Came a squawk.

She turned to face Agnes the crow, which seemed to twitch, its wings outstretched.

'Agnes?' She said.

Its name was its cue to flap, frantically so. Agnes remained fixed to its faux branch, but tried desperately to break free, squawking insanely. Lucille had no time to dwell on the miracle, another, gruffer voice interrupted her.

'If you run or hide or stand or sit...' Said Fernando, a mounted deer head that swung its antlers furiously, smacking at the wall either side of it.

Suddenly there was a monstrous chorus as more and more of the dead creatures reanimated. Ferrets, stoats, foxes, rats, all breaking free and fleeing into dark corners where Lucille would lose sight of them. A few birds loosed there shackles and flew freely, circling their owner, tearing at her with tiny talons. She struck out with her arms, closed her eyes and moved clumsily to where she imagined the hallway to be.

'A bitter wind, pass plain and clod...' Squeaked one of the rodents.

She felt fur at her feet, then teeth, sinking into her calves and ankles. It was Arthur and a few of his friends stripping her flesh, drawing her blood and finally tripping her, causing her to hit her head on a table as she fell. Writhing in agony, she squirmed inching ever closer to the hall, struggling under the weight of the critters. She tried to scream, but as she opened her mouth, a blackbird flew in, wedging itself and drowning her call. Arthur made his way across her chest, deciding to stand on her throat, front paws dug into her cheeks. His eyes were dark and hollow, his mouth frayed where it had once been stitched closed. Arthur looked into Lucille's eyes as he spoke.

'You're on your own... No hope... No...'

He was cut short.

'What the fuck!?' Cried Rufus, standing in the doorway.

Arthur was once again inanimate, the room quiet. Lucille's taxidermy collection was now still, but Rufus caught sight of a few dead birds falling from the air, some loosed feather floating to the ground.

'What the fuck is all this? Are you okay?' He asked, moving to Lucille's aid.

She knocked Arthur to one side then wretched as she pulled the stuffed bird from her mouth, spitting out filth as Rufus lifted her head.

'My god...' She coughed.

'Look at you, you're bleeding,' He propped her up against the wall, 'How did you do this?'

'Demons, Demons!' She wailed.

Rufus noticed the animals, now in vicious poses, not like they were at breakfast, and they were placed around Lucille like they were ready to pounce. This wasn't something she imagined in her lunacy, it wasn't possible. He had seen the birds fall as he entered the room, he was sure of it. This was a diorama too elaborate for Lucille to stage. Her legs were mangled, shredded, and blood was everywhere. He'd heard all the commotion in the first place, it was what brought him downstairs. Whatever had happened here was out of her control, and it had scared her half to death.

'We need to get you some help.'

'How could they? Demons, all of them.' She mumbled.

'Can you stand?'

'My babies, I loved them all.'

'Can you hear me, lady?'

'Thank you,' She sobbed, 'Thank you.'

'It's okay, now come on,' Rufus pulled her to her feet, placing her arm over his shoulder. 'we need to get you some help alright.'

Lucille hopped as best she could, wincing with each stride, Rufus took the brunt of the weight as he helped her into the hall and onto a chair. He picked up the phone behind the reception counter and listened for a dial tone. The storm must have been worse than he thought, the phone was dead. He tapped the switch hook several times, but still no sound.

'The phone isn't working.'

'No, it never does, not on nights like this.'

'Is there a doctor in the village?'

Lucille didn't respond, she just shook her head and wept.

'Hey!' He yelled. 'You're losing a lot of blood here, we need a doctor.'

'There is a doctor, Doctor Henhauser, but I don't need help, just let me rest a moment.'

'Yes you do,' Rufus made his way upstairs, 'I'll be back in a moment, try to stay awake.'

'Stacey!' Called Rufus, as he thumped on her door.

He could hear the sound of unenthusiastic feet dragging across the floor. Stacey, swung open the door, her face a bizarre mix of tired and furious.

'What the fuck do you want?' She breathed.

'I need your help, you need to come downstairs right now.' He blurted.

'You can swivel.'

'Look, you need to help me, this isn't about us.'

'Everything is about you, you shit!'

Rufus had no time for this, he grabbed Stacey's arm and dragged her into the hall.

'Take your fucking hands off me.'

'I'm sorry.'

He pulled her down the stairs, his grip tight and though she struggled, it didn't falter him none.

'You're hurting me, I'll scream.' She whimpered.

'So scream.'

She took in a breath, ready to let loose when she was halted, noticing a passed out Lucille in the hall.

'What happened to her?' She asked, now free of Rufus' grip.

'I don't know, but I need you here, you need to keep her awake.'

'How?'

'I don't know, talk to her, shake her... Slap her if you have to!' Rufus moved to the front door. 'I'm going to find the doctor, I'll be back with help as soon as I can.'

Stacey replied with a humble nod as she placed her arm across Lucille's back. She watched Rufus - who was dressed in only shorts and a thin t-shirt - brave the chaos outside. He'd opened the door and was met by a storm, that soaked him before he'd even stepped out onto the street.

The storm moved in fast. Finn and Jessica had bought a bottle of whisky and found a peak on the moors to settle on for the night. They had sat and enjoyed just one bitter swig when the rain forced them out. Finn held his jacket over her head as they ran, heading for the blurred lights of Golgothaan. They hadn't realised just how far they'd walked, fun and flirtation had lightened the load, sped up time.

As they ran, they laughed, excited despite the ice water running down their collars. Finn noticed something raised in the grass, though it was dark, a geometric silhouette stood out among the sweeping hills. It was clearly manmade, and much closer than the village. As far as Finn was concerned it was civilization.

'Over here!' He yelled.

He pointed to the box, Jessica nodded, though it was hard to see in the confusion. She led the way, pulling Finn by his arm.

It was a small shed of some kind, half buried into the ground with one long, narrow hole across the front. Searching the structure, Jessica found a small door that they could reach via a slope. She tugged on it but it refused to budge, it's hinges rusted solid. Finn took this opportunity to assert himself, his masculinity in dire need of some kind of display. He moved her aside and gripped the handle, then pulled with everything he had. Thank god, he thought as it swung open.

It was dark, but it was dry, and though they could feel the occasional cobweb in their hair, it was preferable to outside. Jessica searched blindly, feeling around on the floor and sides for something she could use.

'Ah ha!' Said Jessica as she stopped rummaging.

There was a click and suddenly Finn was blind, for a moment at least. Jessica held a torch that she moved away from Finn's face just as soon as she knew where it was. She sat it on a small wooden box so it was facing the ceiling, which lit the shed reasonably well.

'Good work.' He said.

'Why thank you.' Said Jessica as she did an exaggerated bow.

'What is this place, a shed? Why would they build a shed all the way out here?'

'It's not a shed you idiot, it's a hide. For bird watching.'

Jessica pointed the torch at the far wall, illuminating a wall chart full of different birds.

'How'd you know that?'

'Because *I'm* smart, Finn.' She boasted. 'Don't you ever read a book?'

'Yeah, course I do, sci-fi stuff mostly, horror now and then.'

Jessica sat down, huge smile on her face.

'Tell me I'm not stuck in here all night with a sci-fi nerd!' She jested.

'Tell me you're not surprised!' Chuckled Finn as he sat down next to her. 'I have geek written all over me.'

'Yeah,' Jessica took his hand, 'You do.'

If there was ever a time, then this was it. The half light did nothing to hide her beauty, in fact it somehow amplified it. Highlighting her features; her delicate nose, her tender lips, the single line under each eye that Finn found adorable. Now, as she stared into his eyes, he could feel himself drawn to her, the pull of her lips beckoning his. He'd seen this before, countless times on film and television, he acted accordingly, plunging forward and meeting her halfway.

A kiss is never just a kiss. His hands found her side, and felt all they could there until it was time to move on. The next place was her front, and as risky as the move was, he took the chance, clasping at her humble breasts as if they were the first he'd ever felt. Jessica pushed him away, though her expression was not that of disgust. She found it amusing.

'Whoa there mister,' She took his busy hand once more. 'I'm not gonna sleep with you in a filthy shed!'

'You said it was a hide.'

'A shed, a hide, you aint getting lucky in either.'

Finn wasn't offended, in fact he respected her for it. The day had shown her in many lights, and each offered him a view into the woman she was. Deep down he knew she'd never go for this, but being male, he couldn't help himself. They both faced each other, holding each other's hands and sharing a peaceful smile. This was enough for him, for now. Though it was cold, and a little wet, the noise from outside had muted, their moment overriding the storm, and both of them prayed that it would last, an excuse for them to remain hidden, together forever.

This had to be it, it had surgery written above the door, though it was hard for Rufus to read anything with so much water in his eyes. The door was unlocked, the villagers of Golgothaan, as backwards as they seemed, trusted one another. He burst in, thankful to be free of the barrage.

'Hello?' He called out.

There came no reply. The hall was a makeshift waiting room, unmatched chairs placed along its sides. A light came from a room further down, the only light source in the house. Rufus headed towards it, cautious in the strange surroundings, it was after all Dr Henhauser's home when it wasn't a surgery.

'Dr Henhauser?' He said, as he approached what looked like his office.

Still no reply, but there was the sound of movement, a gentle rustle. There was a desk in the room, informative medical posters on the wall, and shelves full of apparatus. The shelves had been disturbed, and some equipment lay on the floor, some tools that would seem lethal outside of a doctor's office. The black leather chair behind the desk was still spinning gently. Whoever was here, hadn't been gone for long.

Rufus followed the trail of medical paraphernalia that led him through to a back room, then to some stone stairs, leading to what he imagined was a basement. There was definite movement down there, and a sensation that he couldn't explain. It was like he was entering a room full of generators, the tingle in his chest that he could only approximate to being near electricity, a lot of electricity.

The first thing he saw was a shoe, but whoever it belonged to wasn't standing, he was laying down. Rufus skipped the last few steps, hurrying his decent, immediately regretting his pace when he'd reached the ground.

The white coat suggested to him that it was Henhauser, but the dignity that married it was lost. Henhauser was face down, limbs at awkward angles, angles that only the dead could maintain. He became a statue at the bottom of the stairwell, but it wasn't the corpse that froze him, it was his very reality being shattered. There had been strangeness already tonight; the ornamental birds falling, the aggressive poses of the animals around Lucille. He felt that - in time - it could have been explained away somehow. There was no explaining this.

Henhauser, though dead, was moving. The body was being dragged, slowly towards a hole in the ground. The movers were not of this world, ethereal forms, horrifying shadows that seemed to emanate dread. The very air around them rippled like heat rising from a desert road, but the air was ice. The forms could have been the shadows of men, but they refracted and reformed constantly.

Rufus was tough, he truly believed that there wasn't a fight on earth that he would back down from, but this wasn't of this earth, it was otherworldly. He could do nothing but watch the mob feed Henhauser to the pit, standing perfectly still despite the spasm of his heart. The entities didn't seem to react to him, perhaps they hadn't noticed him, but beings like this were surely aware.

As the Doctor slipped into the dark, a trapdoor slammed shut, sealing him in, then a large refrigerator was slid, effortlessly, over the door. This was probably how the room was before, the door hidden from sight, perhaps there without Henhauser ever knowing it. The basement floor was solid stone, grey and covered in grit, and where Rufus had first saw the doctor lay, hovered a shadow. The stone was chipped away, bit by bit, forming words; *Frank William Henhauser, murdered on this spot 2013*. The words were crude, but etched deep with what seemed to be no effort in such a hard material.

What was to happen now? Their job seemed to be done and all that was left was to be noticed. A witness to their murder, and what usually happened to witnesses if the murderers could manage it? Rufus felt a chill across the back of his neck.

'Why are you here?' Came a whisper.

Rufus didn't react, didn't move. Only he's eyes showed any sign of life, as they glazed, as single tear breaking free.

'I don't know who you are.' The voice was airy, almost like the wind over the moors.

Whatever it was, it moved around Rufus, it presence leaving a trail of cold that seemed to hang.

'It saddens me that I never will.'

The threat caused Rufus to turn, facing the ghost, examining the face of his would-be killer. It was grey, it's face misshapen like the shadows, but it had more form; deep hollowed eyes, black as black could be, remnants of hair on its head, parted in a fashion. Its neck was thin and it sunk into the collar of a white shirt. He couldn't be sure but the entity seemed to be dressed for a funeral, but every time its form came into focus, it was only for a moment, offering snippets of its former self.

Starting in his feet, he felt some life. Adrenaline fuelled his legs, gave him the start he needed to run. He bounded the stairs, three steps at a time, the ghosts in his wake refusing to give chase. He'd made it to the office, then the waiting room and still felt nothing behind him. The front door was still open, the storm outside had never seemed so inviting. He sprinted, the street just one stride away when the door slammed shut, Rufus' nose bursting with blood as he made contact with it. He fell to the floor, dazed and half blind.

'How can you escape us?' Whispered the dead man, his voice seemingly everywhere. 'How can you escape the wind, the very air. We are in your lungs, we are in your blood...'

'What are you?' Whimpered Rufus.

'We are beyond definition!' It roared.

They allowed him no response, no reaction. The shadows crept out from every corner, surrounding Rufus and raising him into the air like he was paper-light. They pulled his legs and arms in directions they were never meant to bend, contorted his body in ways he never thought possible. They tugged with a force that he thought couldn't last, the elasticity of his limbs being enough to hold him together as long as this was all they had. It wasn't. They didn't falter, instead they pulled and pulled, effortlessly. He couldn't scream so much as croak, his throat taught, his windpipe closed. This was no cramp, he'd suffered plenty of those, this was a pain that promised more pain to come, until the final snap. There was the sound of loosened Velcro, a relief that he now welcomed as he was torn to pieces, blood and gore spraying the hall as his torso fell, seconds before his arms, legs and head.

3

Another dead end, a slope with no footing, just muck that slid and squirmed underfoot. Eugene felt his age, wheezing as he walked, he must have walked miles to no avail, in circles most likely. Refusing to quit he endured, searching the next tunnel he crossed, praying that it was not one he'd already investigated.

It was quite the labyrinth under Golgothaan, but its purpose was no less a mystery than when he was dumped here. The skulls - though sporadic - still watched from the mud walls, but their effect had lessened as exhaustion took over. Given enough time, even terror will subside, when no other option is available but to confront it, the mystery would lose some of its grip. The unknown is what truly terrifies most, but the unknown had lost its potency with Eugene, forced to be victim to it for hours now.

The stench of the tunnels didn't even register now, that was until he made one more turn, tried yet another tunnel, following a much stronger scent. At first glance it was just another tunnel, same as all the others, but as he proceeded he noticed something, the cause of the foul smell. There were less skulls here, but there was one different from the others; a skull with marbled flesh, bleached eyes and matted hair. Eugene recognized the face, seen it briefly at the Ashen Maid, it was Larry Mumford, embedded in the mud, just his agonized face protruding. The wall was newly formed around him, recently impacted and molded to shape.

It was just another surprise that the catacombs had to offer, as shocking as it was, Eugene failed to mourn the man. He was more intrigued than afraid, and it occurred to him that there were probably skeletons behind all of the skulls he'd passed, buried in the walls.

He didn't have time to hang around, a gust of wind forced him to move, and an ominous presence that proceeded it encouraged him to move further. The lights dimmed as a mass of shadows approached, completely darkening the path behind it. It rushed like water in a pipe at a speed that Eugene wasn't sure he couldn't match. He tried nonetheless, galloping with all he had, one hand clasping his aching hip.

For once in what felt like a lifetime he had a stroke of luck, surely the divine intervention of the Lord himself; a door at the end of the tunnel. It was wooden, rotten and crudely fitted, but it meant that another soul had been here. As he slammed into it, he didn't waste a moment looking behind him, how would that help? The shadows were coming whether he checked or not, he needed every second.

The iron handle was damp - like everything else - and it slipped out of his hand, the weight unexpected. He tried again, composed under the circumstances, and felt some give in the door. One more tug and it was open, no sooner than he was through it and slamming it shut behind him. It didn't matter where he was, anything was preferable to the horror that would be knocking any moment now.

He could hear it, the deafening whoosh and hiss of it, the choir of moans and wails. It was a force of its own, changing the very atmosphere. Yet it refused to follow him in, halting at the door before finally turning away. Eugene was still alive, despite everything Golgothaan had to throw at him.

'It won't be long, he should be back soon.' Said Stacey, knelt on the floor by Lucille.

'He really needn't bother, I'm over the worst of it now.'

'Well some of these cuts seem pretty nasty,' Stacey stood up. 'do you have any plasters, bandages, a medical kit or something?'

Lucille nodded to the reception counter.

'There's a box behind there.'

Stacey made her way over, lifting the countertop and stepping in.

'You can't go back there, that's for employees only.'

'Yeah, sure.' Said Stacey, as she rummaged around on the shelves. 'When was the last time you cleaned back here Miss Tourney?'

'It's clean enough!' She barked.

She'd found a green box, caked in dust, then returned to Lucille.

'Clean enough, eh?'

She held up the box and blew the dust off, the cloud making Lucille wince. Inside were a few plasters, bandages and iodine, the gear was ancient.

'We're gonna clean some of these cuts, okay?' Said Stacey, antiseptic in hand.

Lucille didn't squirm, she allowed Stacey to help, accepting that her first opinion of her and her friends may have been wrong.

'You're a good girl,' She said, 'I'm grateful for you and your friend's help. It's very Christian of you.'

'Don't mention it, I'm sure you'd do the same.'

Lucille contemplated the statement.

'I don't know about that, living on your own like I do, you tend to lose faith in everything but the good book.'

'That's no way to live.'

'Maybe you're right.'

Stacey begun to wrap a bandage around her leg, trying her best to remember what she'd learned on a childcare course she'd taken once upon a time. She changed her career choices like she did her men. On another night, in a different situation, she may have found the course, black hairs on Lucille's legs repulsive, recoiling in her shallow way. But not tonight, she felt a maturity tonight that she hadn't experienced before in her pampered little life.

'Can I ask, Lucille, what happened? How did this happen to you?'

Lucille shook her head, hardly believing it herself anymore.

'My pets, the animals in the breakfast room, they attacked me.'

'Is that right?' Mocked Stacey.

'You don't have to believe me, child, convincing you is not a concern of mine.'

It was ludicrous, and she would be an idiot to believe otherwise, but the cuts were definitely scratches and bites of some kind. Stacey tried to imagine how else they could have been made, finally accepting the fact that she wasn't smart enough to figure any of this out.

'Where the hell is he?' She muttered. 'How long can it take?'

Lucille placed her hands on Stacey's cheeks, gently lifting her head to face her.

'I won't have been the only one, not tonight. Golgothaan isn't safe, child, no one here is safe!'

Stacey froze, caught in Lucille's gaze. Though she didn't believe the words, it was alarming to look into the eyes of someone who truly did.

'What is wrong with this place?' She whispered.

Lucille took a defeated breath.

'My dear... Golgothaan is like monkshood. Beautiful on the surface, but deep down, at its roots... There's death!.'

It was some kind of a study, hidden away under the earth. The floor was covered in wooden planks, allowing Eugene some welcomed footing. There were bookcases, chests, tables and other furniture lined up along the walls. In the centre of the room was a desk, large and elaborate, clearly the centerpiece, its detail striking against the simplicity of the dirt walls.

The room hadn't been used in decades, the smell of damp emanating from the books and papers, still placed neatly on the shelves. It was a slice of morbid comfort, in the middle of a nightmare.

An inquisitive soul, Eugene brushed his finger along the shelves, examining everything he pointed to. His attention was drawn to the centre desk, that had a single book resting on top of it. Leather-bound and sturdy, it had the words *Henrick Baines' Journal* embossed on its cover. He wasn't sure whether to touch it or not, a journal is private, whether its subject is alive or not.

A studded leather chair was tucked into the desk and Eugene couldn't resist it, his hip begging for rest. As he sat he felt he like would never stand up again, the relief was the closest he'd felt to bliss in a long time. His eyelids were heavy, but he tried everything he could to stay awake, sleep was most certainly death in this place. In his drowsy state he slid the journal closer, his need to remain conscious outweighing the privacy of a dead man.

The book had kept well. It wasn't nearly as musty as it should have been, the pages were intact and the cover, though weighty, was as fixed as the day it was bound. Eugene started at page one, treating it as a novel, which as he read on, became a book more intriguing than any novel he'd ever read before.

How they ever managed to sleep was a mystery, but they woke up, propped against the hide's wall, Jessica's head buried in Finn's chest. Their muscles ached, their bones were taught, but the night was the best they'd had in a while. Sun poured in through the opening, highlighting just how dirty their lodgings were, sunbeams given shape thanks to floating motes.

'Good morning.' Whispered Finn, as he noticed Jessica stir.

He brushed the hair from her face, touching her made it all real to him.

'Jeez, I feel like a cat shit in my mouth.' She grunted.

Finn laughed.

'Not much of a morning person?'

'Not usually, especially with half a bottle of whiskey in me.'

'Surprisingly, I feel fine.'

'Well bully for you,' She tapped his chin, gently with her finger, 'what time is it?'

'I have no idea, my phone died long ago.'

Jessica rummaged in her pocket, slid out her phone and checked the screen.

'Seven missed calls, all from Stacey.'

She placed it back into her jeans.

'Aren't you going to call her back?'

'Hell no! Spoil this beautiful morning!? She probably wanted someone to moan at, about your friend most likely.'

'He can be a dick sometimes.'

'Well, so can she.'

Jessica looked up, smiled and then pecked Finn on the lips. He'd woken up, hoping that she wasn't full of regret or shame. The kiss helped quash his doubts.

'We better get back, they will be wondering where we've gotten too.' Suggested Finn.

'You're probably right, and I don't know about you, but I could use a nice, warm, shower.'

The pair stood up, helping each other at some effort, the result of an awkward night's sleep causing them both to grimace and groan.

Temporarily blinded as they wedged open the door, the morning sun felt like a welcomed luxury after the weather they'd been having. It was hard to believe that the sky had ever been darkened by storm clouds, hardly a wisp of white in the sky now, just endless blue heading off to sea.

The peace of the moors was sorely missed as Finn and Jessica entered Golgothaan. There was some kind of impromptu town meeting; a small crowd of twenty or so villagers, gathered by the Ashen Maid, hanging on Father Hogan's every word. They were huddled like lost sheep, and Hogan was to be their shepherd.

'What is this?' Asked Finn.

'I don't know, but I'm in no state to care.' Said Jessica, 'Let's try and give them the slip.'

Finn nodded. They both tried to pass by, nonchalantly, creeping in a cartoon-like fashion. They heard some of Hogan's speech as they crept.

'People, please, we must not jump to conclusions. I admit, the turnout here today is somewhat less than usual, but until anything turns up, nothing is certain.' Hogan held out his hands. 'We must not fall apart, unity is what makes this village great...'

'Unity!? My wife is gone, that was the only unity I gave a shit about!' Said a large man in the crowd.

'We don't know that she's dead, Patrick. As I said before, nothing is certain.'

The debate caught their attention, Jessica and Finn stopped and hung around at the back.

'We know they're dead Father, we just know.' Came a woman, sobbing into a handkerchief.

'All I'm trying to do here is preach faith, trust in our lord, his ways...'

'That's all you ever do, *preach faith*, what use is faith to us now?' Growled Patrick.

'Faith is everything, especially in times like these, don't you ever forget that.'

'It's fine for Father Hogan,' Said another man, directing it at the crowd, 'he has no one to lose, he doesn't know our pain.'

The crowd mumbled in agreement.

'You may be right, but I am no stranger to loss, I'm not oblivious to your suffering.'

'If you weren't oblivious, you wouldn't be spouting this rubbish.' Said the sobbing woman.

Father Hogan was in over his head, beads of sweat formed on his brow that he wiped casually, hoping to assure the mob of his confidence.

'What the hell is going on?' Whispered Jessica.

'I have no idea, but it seems pretty serious.' Replied Finn.

The crowd were talking amongst themselves, moaning and complaining, the noise drowning out the priest as he tried desperately them win back.

'Your loved ones are dead!' Yelled a woman, making her way, slowly, to the gathering.

Everyone turned to see Lucille - Looney Lucille as she was known - who limped with purpose, despite the pain that was clearly expressed on her face. Behind her followed an embarrassed stranger, a young girl who clearly didn't belong. Usually, any statement from Lucille would have been immediately dismissed, but this time it was different, the people were desperate for answers, even if they were to come from a loon.

'Please Lucille, this isn't helping.' Said Father Hogan.

'Let her speak!' Demanded someone in the crowd.

She was suddenly overwhelmed. The attention of anyone, let alone a crowd, was something she hadn't experienced in years. Lucille knew what people thought of her, though she never could understand their repulsion. The crazy never know that they're crazy, and each dismissal or insult had an effect on her. No matter how oblivious they thought she was, her emotions functioned just as everyone else's did. She would often get hurt and return to her home alone, the consolation of loved ones was only a dream to her.

'We're all going to die here!' She said, shakily. 'Golgothaan is going to swallow us whole!'

'What is this nonsense, I suggest you keep your paranoid delusions to yourself.' Protested Hogan.

'Shut up priest!' Barked Stacey, defending her new friend.

Jessica gestured to Stacey, inviting her over. She wasted no time, galloping, relieved to see a familiar face.

'If you truly follow the good book, Father, then you should believe in it.' Said Lucille.

'So you're going to teach *me* about the good book now? What could *Loony* Lucille possibly have to teach me, *a priest*, about the good book?'

'If you believe, I mean truly believe, then you need to accept that while there are angels, the holy spirit and everything else that is good, then you would be an fool to ignore all that is evil.'

A few of the crowd members were cautiously nodding, while others were lost, hoping that it would all become clear soon enough.

'I'm not entirely sure what you're getting at here, Lucille.'

'Demons, evil spirits, they're real, and Golgothaan is home to an ungodly horde.'

Father Hogan was lost for words, truly worried for Lucille's state of mind.

'She has been talking about this stuff all night.' Said Stacey, 'I have no idea what's going on! Lucille, the lodge owner, has been swearing blind that she was attacked by, and you're never gonna believe this, her stuffed animal collection!'

'What the hell?' Said Jessica.

'Tell me about it! Meanwhile, I've had to stay up all night, clean her wounds and make sure she doesn't fall asleep.'

'Where's Rufus?' Asked Finn.

'I have no idea, the shit bag left me with Lucille, told me some bullshit about going to fetch the doctor. The doctor must live in John O' Groats or something 'cos he still isn't back.'

Finn screwed up his face and shook his head in disbelief.

'This isn't like him. Not like him at all.' Said Finn. 'I mean he'd go home with a girl, be gone for a day, two at the most, but he would never have left Lucille, not if it was bad.'

'Well,' Said Stacey, eyes wide, 'he did!'

Jessica scanned the crowd, remembering their complaints, and the fact that Rufus may have not been the only one to disappear last night.

'I don't want to worry you Finn, but a lot of people went missing last night.' Said Jessica, stroking Finn's shoulder with her hand. 'I shouldn't even say it, but maybe Rufus, is...'

'What, gone!?' Snapped Finn. 'Because everyone else here is convinced that they're dead. Not gone, dead!'

'I'm sorry, I'm just trying to rationalize all this. Anyway, if they *were* dead, there would be bodies, blood... Something.'

Finn was clearly worried.

'Look, I'm gonna go check my room, see if his stuff is there.' He said as he started moving away.

'Do you want me to come with you?' Asked Jessica.

'No, it's fine, you stay here, I'll only be a minute or two.'

Finn was out of earshot before Jessica could say anything else. She looked at her friend, who seemed frustratingly indifferent to Finn's concern. Stacey was more intrigued as to what had happened to her friend last night, astounded by Jessica's body language, her sudden comfort with Finn. She had a sixth sense for things like this.

The crowd were torn, and it had become apparent that those who believed Lucille's tale were those that had experienced otherworldly occurrences the night before. None of the experiences were to the extent of hers, but those that were already superstitious, didn't need much convincing. Those that experienced it had only experienced the echo of something supernatural, never the actual act. Unlike Lucille, who was saved from certain death by an outsider, someone who was never supposed to be in Golgothaan.

Father Hogan protested till the end, finally walking away and back to his church. He wasn't missed, most didn't even notice him leave. The village told their stories, their brushes with the paranormal, each so convinced that their conviction spread like a virus. It wasn't long before small village mentality took over and a mob was formed. Short of fire and pitchforks they were ready to face whatever the next storm might bring.

The door to the room was open, Rufus must have left in a hurry. His things were still there, his bed unmade. Somehow Finn knew that the room was going to be this way before he'd even walked in. Something in his gut had told him so, a sinking feeling of dread, the village seemed rife with it today.

Sat on the edge of his bed, he examined the room, looking for clues while having absolutely no idea what a clue might be. Rufus was dead, he was sure of it, even though there was no evidence, his paranoia, that would make anything terrible a certainty, had returned. His time with Jessica had changed him, seemed to sedate his neuroses, but like any sedation it was beginning to wear off. Like numbed pain, when it returns, it seemed more potent than it ever was before.

While lost in thought, Finn hadn't realised just how quiet the empty building was, so quiet that when the smallest of sounds took place, it snapped him from his trance. It was a delicate tap on the hardwood floor in the hall, a gentle patter that made its way to his room.

Surely this was a hallucination, Finn had to shake his head and wipe his eyes. A slick, black head showed itself in the open doorway. Small and close to the ground, it stared at Finn with dark eyes, seemingly as inquisitive as he was. It was an otter, squeaking at Finn, inviting him to follow. How could he refuse, the oddity begged curiosity, especially one as adorable as Arthur the otter.

Finn stood up and took a few gentle steps towards the animal, it looked up, sniffed the air and then headed off down the hall. He quickened his pace, trying to keep up with the critter who would turn a corner as soon as Finn thought he'd caught up. Following the squeaks, he ended up in the breakfast room. Lucille's taxidermy collection was in tatters, scattered across the floor, the odd table flipped on its side. He looked the room over, but his attention was drawn to the rustling bead curtain, swinging as if something small had just crawled under it. He didn't notice Arthurs old stand, the wooden block with four dust free patches where his paws once were.

He parted the beads and entered the kitchen, finally catching up to Arthur who was scratching furiously at the black and white check linoleum.

'Hey, little fella, what are you doing there?' He asked as he inched ever closer.

The otter wasn't distracted by his approach, it continued to scratch and gnaw at the floor, tearing up strips and revealing the wooden planks underneath. When Finn was close enough, he held out his arm to touch the creature, hoping to assure himself that this wasn't a vivid and very lucid daydream. As he made contact with the otter's old, dry fur, it turned like a flash, snapping at his fingers, drawing blood in an instant. He recoiled, letting out a subdued yowl.

'What the fuck was that for?' He growled.

Arthur returned to his work, revealing more and more of the floor underneath the linoleum, shredding at it with an unnatural ferocity. Finn stood over it, curiosity keeping him there, making him watch. He was certain that there was a reason for the otter, and that whatever was under the kitchen floor, was something that he had to see.

Arthur had finished, revealing what seemed to be a trapdoor, then backed away. He chirped, inviting Finn over to investigate. Finn couldn't help himself, and somehow felt that he was being offered a clue into the disappearance of his friend. He wondered if Lucille knew about this hidden door, it was hidden well and the linoleum flooring seemed almost as old as the wood underneath.

'What is this?' Asked Finn, the otter offering the only blank expression it had.

A cold draft rose from its seams. Finn held his hand over the cracks, the chill was felt deeper than his palms, it was felt in his veins, flowing right to his heart. The ominous sensation was warning enough to run away, but his arm had a momentum of its own, clasping a sunken handle and pulling open the door. It coughed as a stench was released, forcing Finn to step back.

The otter wasted no time, he leapt straight into the seemingly endless black without a sound. Finn felt like he should follow Arthur, his instincts screaming *jump*. His curiosity ended there, despite what his body wanted, he knew that it was death down there, the odour was testament to that.

The front door was opened, he could hear it from the kitchen, the snap of the bolt made his heart thud. Finn nervously called out

'Hello!' but there came no reply. Footsteps approached from the hall, then from the breakfast room. Eventually the footsteps were just a beaded curtain away.

The tension was quashed as a head of copper coloured hair made its way through the beads. It was Jessica, he would recognise that colour anywhere; a mix of auburn and light brown, a colour all of its own, as unique as Jessica was. Finn's body went from ice to warm water in an instant.

'Thank god.' He whispered to himself.

'What are you doing in here?' Asked Jessica.

She stepped into the kitchen, followed shortly by Stacey who grimaced at the decor.

'You scared the life out of me.' He chuckled.

Finn smiled, relieved to see Jessica, glad to have some human company. He watched the girls who seemed to ignore him, each staring, eyes huge. They watched the space above his head, their faces taught with what could only be horror. It was no joke, they were not actors, they were petrified and whatever it was that paralyzed them was looming above him. He could feel it, the vibration of it. It was the sensation of touching water and not knowing for a moment if it was too hot or too cold.

'Finn...' Whimpered Jessica.

He found it difficult to take his eyes off Jessica, feeling like she would disappear if he were to turn away for a second.

'What is it?' He demanded.

'Finn!' She screamed.

It forced him to turn to face an amorphous shadow, billowing from the pit. It towered over him, casting him in shade. It stirred and twitched in a constant battle to keep its shape. He didn't have long to comprehend it (it would have taken a lifetime) before it smothered him, cloaking him in darkness. It retracted, returning to the hole as quickly as a rubber band snapping, taking Finn with it.

It took only a second, the door slamming shut behind it. Jessica's reaction was delayed, numbed by terror. She leapt forward much too late, screaming Finn's name, and as she scrambled towards the trapdoor she was knocked aside by a hurtling bread bin. The piece of kitchen furniture cleared her out of the way as everything else in the kitchen moved. A small table, a chair, drawers, cupboards and even the oven, all flew towards the trapdoor, pulled like dust into a vacuum cleaner. The furniture smashed and shattered, creating a barricade that made sure no one else was getting into the pit.

Jessica rubbed her shoulder, dazed by the collision. She crawled forward and tried desperately to move the rubble, unable to budge a splinter.

'Don't just stand there, help me!' She yelled.

Stacey was useless now, quivering like a flag in the wind.

There wasn't a chance that she could move the refrigerator, not even with Stacey's help. All she could do was break down, kneeling against the pile and wailing with frustration. Stacey didn't comfort her, she wasn't even aware that her friend was crying, all she could see was the black cloud. The reality-shattering shadow that could only have been death itself.

What was a shepherd without his flock? Father Hogan was back where he belonged, in his church, moving from pew to pew, picking up the bibles that had been placed so delicately. The Lady on the Moors was empty and silent, only his steps could be heard on the tiles. He liked this, escaping the villagers, those that would usually adore him. Despite his baser urges - those that were forbidden in his line of work - He was happy to be alone and unattached. It was only when he'd walk the empty aisle that he'd realize just how much solitude suited him.

Perhaps, being alone meant that he had nothing to prove, no one to satisfy, unlike the meeting earlier today when so many depended on him. The job required him to care, constantly, which he'd soon discovered, early on in his priesthood, was exhausting.

Father Hogan believed that he had a calling, and never in his years had he doubted the existence of God, but he often doubted that this was where he should be. Often feeling like an imposter, he felt that it was only a matter of time before he was found out for the fraud he was.

It had been a bad day, he was bound to doubt himself. Whenever he'd feel sorry for himself, he'd remember just how lucky he was to be posted here, in this church. It's beauty never becoming familiar, always seeming new.

The windows, stained in a hundred different colours, were positioned perfectly above the pulpit to catch the afternoon sun. A rainbow lay across the aisle. Thomas stepped into it, examining his arm that was illuminated stunningly, the colours resting on his pale hand.

He looked up to the light, contemplating what Lucille had said, trying his best to consider the strange happenings in Golgothaan and whether there was any truth to their stories. He couldn't bring himself to believe in ghosts and monsters, but how can so many be so convinced, and in the space of one night no less.

Thomas found himself asking for answers, not saying a word out loud, just countless words in his head. Staring at where he imagined God to be, usually where the light was brightest, he would stand for minutes at a time.

Deep in prayer, he heard a voice. Opening his eyes he expected to see an angel, or heavenly messenger of some sort, there to finally answer his call. This was not the case, and the voice was not ethereal but disappointingly human. It was muffled, and its source was hidden, so he called out to it, hoping to pinpoint where it was. Whatever it was, it was in need of help, this much was clear.

'Hello?' He yelled.

The voice became louder, reacting to Father Hogan's call. Suddenly there was a thudding sound, the sound of knuckles on concrete. Hogan moved to the end of the church hall, past the pulpit and overly elaborate organ. The sounds were close and at his feet. More confused than afraid he lay the bibles on the floor with care and called out once more.

'Hello? Where are you?'

He could make out words now, words that were coming from the ground, below a marble slab that vibrated slightly with each thump.

'Help me...' Came the voice. 'Get me out of here...'

'Why are you in my floor?' He asked, ridiculously.

'Get me out... Please God, get me out!'

Hogan knelt, feeling for a gap wide enough for his fingers. As he found a spot, he shook his head, ashamed to be humouring the talking floor tile. The marble was heavy, barely moving at all in the soft grip of the priest.

'You need to push, on the count of three, okay?'

'Okay,' Said the muffled voice.

'One... Two... Three!'

As the slab raised slightly, he managed to get both hands under it, not considering the potential crushing of his bones if the person underneath was to let go.

'Keep pushing, don't you dare stop!' He begged.

He had to think fast, struggling under the weight, being a priest he had no need for physical strength. One of the bibles he'd collected was not too far from reach, he scooped it with his foot, kicking it over. In one quick motion he grabbed it with one freed hand and slid it into the gap. The slab fell onto the bible, which held, giving his hands a much welcomed rest. His hands had never known calluses, and if he could help it, they never would.

In the dark he could see wild, desperate eyes. It was in his nature to try and lift the slab once more, letting out whoever was trapped underneath, but he hesitated. Accepting the fact that there was a man under the church floor suddenly becoming too much.

'W-what is this?' He stuttered. 'Who are you?'

Hands found their way through the gap, the fingers saturated with filth, mud wedged under the nails.

'Please, let me out...' Wheezed the man in the floor. 'I've come so far!'

'Tell me who you are, you have to understand how bizarre this is for me. There is a man... In my floor!'

The stranger coughed, then took a breath, calming himself enough to explain.

'My name is Eugene Mire, I was staying at the Scarlet Lodge. The reason I'm in your floor is... This is where the tunnel ends!'

'You *can't* go!' Begged Jessica.

'We *can't* stay!' Protested Stacey.

She hadn't even packed her things, she'd grabbed her handbag and ran, dressed only in the vest top and pyjama bottoms she'd put on the night before. It was cold but her car would be warm, warm and safe. Stacey was fleeing, marching down the cobbles with Jessica not far behind, desperate to stop her friend from leaving.

'You can't leave me here, I need you.'

'How can you even think of staying?'

'I can't leave Finn.'

'You don't *even* know him, and...' Stacey waved her arms ridiculously. 'He's fucking gone, Jessica!'

Her car was parked in a small gravel patch near the Ashen Maid, where the only other car was Rufus'. Her shiny, immaculate white BMW Mini, was the closest thing to home right now. She longed to be in it and miles away.

'I won't believe that, I can't.' Jessica caught up to Stacey, who was now searching for car keys in her bag. 'It didn't kill him, you saw it too, it took him down that pit. Maybe they're all down there...'

'Look!' Snapped Stacey, turning to face her. 'He was a fucking stranger, you barely knew him.'

Jessica shook her head in denial.

'I *know* him.' She whimpered.

'No, you didn't.' Stacey was shaking, both furious and terrified. 'You know me, you have *known* me forever...' She placed her hand firmly on Jessica's shoulder, hoping to shake some sense into her. 'I will not die here, like your friend and every other one of these backward fucks!'

'But you would leave me?'

'I don't want too.' Stacey shook her head desperately. 'You should be leaving, with me!'

Jessica's head dropped.

'I can't.'

Stacey had had enough. After what she'd seen today, not even her best friend was going to stop her from escaping. No matter how much it tore her up inside. She found the keys and opened the door, taking one last look at Jessica who stood, red faced, snot-nosed and totally adamant. Stacey knew that there was no budging her.

'You're an idiot.' Said Stacey, as her eyes became damp. 'I can't stay here, Jess, I'm sorry but I, just can't!'

She couldn't stress the words enough.

'Go on, leave.' Said Jessica while wiping her face. 'You don't have to feel bad... I won't blame you for going.'

This was a test, a guilt trip, and as soon as it was tried, it had failed. There wasn't a chance that Stacey would stay, this was clear. Honestly, what normal person would in this situation. Finn *was* a stranger, Stacey was right, but she couldn't leave him. Something in her gut told her that there was hope, she couldn't abandon that feeling, no matter how small it was.

Stacey took Jessica's hand and held it compassionately between both palms.

'I have to go, okay.' She nodded gently. 'I'm so sorry.'

Jessica tried to be strong, not giving Stacey the satisfaction. She slipped her hand free from her friend's and took a step back.

'If you think I'm bringing your things home with me when this is all over, you'll be sorely disappointed.'

This charade was transparent, Stacey knew just how vulnerable her friend was. She had opened the car door and started the engine, the feel of the seat on her back already made her feel safer.

'Leave them, I can always buy more.'

She pulled out of the gravel patch and on to the one road out of Golgothaan. She yelled, 'You're an idiot! Be safe!' as she sped away.

The smaller the car became, the harder she found it to breath, as if her lungs were mirroring it. Jessica was alone, the realisation hitting her hard when Stacey's tiny white car had finally disappeared over a small hill.

She was stranded in a village that was quickly dwindling, without a clue of where to go or what to do next. Turning on the spot she noticed the moors, now cast in shade. The air had become electric, felt only on the delicate hairs on her skin. The storm was returning, rolling faster and thicker than before, drenching the ground and blotting out the sun.

Golgothaan didn't have long. The approaching storm was to be the biggest the village had ever seen. The price of its destruction would be more than a few roof tiles and fallen fence posts. This storm was bringing the promise of death in tow.

4

Though his head was still, his brain continued to swirl. Like the impact of a car crash his organs were still moving, rattling inside him as he was dumped onto the floor. It took moments for the blood to return, his vision, patchy with dark spots, the soundless fizz of pigments that danced in front of his eyes, slowly dissipating as his equilibrium returned. He was left to lay disorientated, in a room that seemed to swell and shrink, like the shallow beat of a dying heart.

The journey had lasted only seconds, but he may have blacked out, he couldn't be sure. The shadow had taken Finn and saw fit to leave him in a strange room, relatively unharmed. As logic returned, he looked around, desperately trying to spot others who had disappeared in the village, assuming that they'd all ended up wherever he was. He hoped to see Rufus most of all, but was bitterly disappointed to be alone.

It was the underground study, the furniture and dirt walls confused Finn as much as it did Eugene, but this time the room seemed to hum. Its walls were moist, slick with grime that slivered like veins across its surface. Finn didn't care to hang around, heading straight for the wooden door that led to the tunnels. The door didn't stick, it opened with ease, but Finn was unable to escape. A miasma of shadows, turbulent yet stationary, blocked his path. It filled the tunnel and remained wedged as if it was waiting for a command to attack.

He slammed the door shut, indifferent to the entity's feelings, the anger it might feel having the door shut in its face. He reacted purely on instinct, and surprisingly to him, his instinct to survive - an instinct that you can never fake or force - was rampant. Finn had always imagined that if the time would ever come where his end was nigh, he would lay down and accept it. Perhaps it was the feelings he'd discovered for Jessica that gave him hope. He found himself thinking of her in his darkest moment, a true sign of what really matters.

Backing away from the door, he heard a voice behind him;

'You shouldn't anger the storm.' Came a whisper. 'It's temperamental, as all storms are.'

Finn spun to confront whoever it was, seeing nobody in the room, just the movement of the chair behind the desk. A form took shape, rippling like disturbed water, sitting casually in the studded leather chair like it belonged there.

'Who's there?' Yelled Finn, his voice trembling.

As the misty figure took a semblance of shape, its voice became louder.

'Are you afraid?'

This was no time for bravado, not with the storm at the door.

'Yes.' He whimpered.

'Do you fear for your life?'

Finn nodded with a quivering lip and a tear in his eye. A tall, thin shadow of a man had manifested itself. Sitting behind the desk, it trailed its fingers through the dust on top, reveling in the sensation of touch, as if it was the first time it had felt anything in a long while.

'Life is just a blink of the eye... Everything to those who have it, nothing to those who don't.'

A chest shook loose from where it had sat for years, sliding across the planks and halting by Finns legs.

'Take a seat.' Said the entity.

Finn didn't react, he stood defiant, suspicious of a trap.

'Sit!' Yelled a hundred voices, all in unison and from every corner of the room.

He did as commanded, dropping onto the chest, his heart dropping much lower.

'Sorry,' Said the man, chuckling quietly to himself. 'I can have a temper too. When your only company is chaos... Restraint, civility, manners... Like whispers in a gale, go unnoticed.'

'W-why have you brought me here?' Whispered Finn.

'To see your face...' The man seemed to swell, distorting slightly as he leaned forward to answer his guest. 'Or rather... Mine!'

The chink of china on china made his teeth grit. The tea set was delicate and Eugene's hands were shaking far too much. He clasped the cup in his palms, the warmth was a welcomed pleasure, leaving the saucer on the table. He sipped, the taste was divine, he swirled it around his gums and teeth, washing away filth that had filled his every pore in the depths. Eugene thought he'd taste nothing but foulness ever again.

He thanked god that he was free, free and in the company of one of his flock. Father Thomas Hogan had been quite the host, helping Eugene to his rectory that sat beside the church, the building was much quainter than its neighbour. It didn't suit the priest, it was much too old fashioned; there were doilies on the surfaces, painted china on the walls, most featuring biblical images, and in some cases, cute cats. The house was immaculate, not an object out of place or an undusted side. Thomas had no desire to make the rectory his own, he accepted it as he did the church, as he did his job. He always saw it as temporary, no matter how many years he'd end up being there.

'I can't thank you enough.' Croaked Eugene, his voice harsh.

'What sort of priest would I be if I were to leave you in the ground?'

Father Hogan sat down, opposite Eugene on a small dining table.

'Not just that, your hospitality, everything.'

'It goes with the job,' Thomas smiled. 'Though I'll admit, this isn't completely altruistic, I need explanations, I do love a good mystery.'

Thomas looked at the book in Eugene's hands, a book that he clutched ever so tightly. He had washed his hands and face, but the book was still caked in mud. When he was helped out of the hole, he had nothing but the soiled clothes on his back and the journal of Henrick Baines. The climb out would have been easier if Eugene had let go of the book, freeing his hand.

'What is that you have there?'

Eugene, held up the book. Crumbs of dried mud fell on to the immaculate table, making Father Hogan wince a little.

'This is everything you need to know, the history of this godforsaken village.'

Hogan read the title of the book.

'Who is Henrick Baines?' He asked.

'He is Golgothaan, it's beginning and its end.'

'*I am the Alpha and Omega, the First and the Last, the Beginning and the End.* Revelations, twenty-two, thirteen.' Thomas smirked. 'That doesn't look like the good book to me.'

'It's far from it... Very far from it.'

Eugene shook his head. Thomas examined his guests solemn expression.

'You believe this stuff don't you, whatever it is in that book. It has really gotten to you.'

'This is no work of fiction, it is a journal, and I know it to be true... I've seen too much.' Said Eugene with utter conviction.

The priest wasn't smiling now, he was concerned, not for Golgothaan, but for the sanity of his guest.

'I want to believe you Eugene,' He lifted the teapot and refilled Eugene's cup. 'Tell me everything you know.'

He took in a breath, preparing himself to share all that he'd read in the hidden study.

'Henrick Baines built Golgothaan, it was his project. You may look around this place, look at the buildings and think, oh what history, what ancient beauty, but you would be wrong. It is all a facade!'

'How can that be?'

'Baines had an ideal, and believe it or not, money was his motive. You have to spend money to make money, this has always been the case, even in 1902 when he started this morbid project of his.' He took a sip to moisten his mouth. 'Tourism was his goal, and though the fortune he spent building this village was more than most would ever see, for Henrick this wasn't enough.

'This is nonsense, the Lady on the Moor has been here for hundreds of years.'

'How can you know that? It's design? I don't know about you, but I couldn't place it, it's a church all of its own.'

Thomas screwed up his face, the point was valid, he had seen his share of churches and none matched the extravagant design of this one.

'Show me this book,' Father Hogan demanded, taking it from Eugene's grip and flipping through the pages, 'this is somebody's idea of a joke... It's just words, Eugene, a story.'

'Henrick Baines is real, he is the evil beneath Golgothaan. *He* is the reason I was under your church, the reason I was put through hell.'

'It was no accident, Finn.' Said the man, his voice often cracking into an ethereal hiss.

'What? What was no accident?' Whimpered Finn.

'You have come home.'

'This is not home, I don't belong here!'

'Foolish boy, why ever else would you come to a place like this?'

He was stumped, his reasons for visiting Golgothaan had always been a mystery. Of all the places to choose from, this village called to him. Its discovery was surely more than coincidence, as obscure and elusive as Golgothaan was, its existence was made blatantly obvious to Finn, and its appeal had become irresistible. Fate had drawn him there, the price of which, was the life of his friend.

'Where is my friend?' Asked Finn, realising that whatever had happened to Rufus, was his fault.

'The coloured fellow?' The man smiled. 'My storm had their way with him, there was no talking them down.'

'He's dead?'

'I'm afraid so, Finn. But know this from someone who really does know... Death is only the beginning.'

Finn could hold back no longer, the realisation of his friends death was breaking point.

'I can't take this anymore, this is insane!' Wailed Finn, head cradled in his hands.

The entity was displeased with the display. His form ruptured, spiking violently, then flew towards Finn, travelling metres in mere moments. The translucent form knocked Finn to the ground, sending him across the planks, then reformed over his aching body, the thin man now straddling the weeping youth. Its voice was now a horrific choir again, terrifying and powerful.

'Stop your whimpering child!' The man's hollow eyes pierced Finns. 'This weakness is a pathetic trait, certainly not of my blood!'

Finn squirmed, struggling fruitlessly under the inhuman force of the man atop him.

'Blood!?' He squealed. 'What blood, what do you mean?'

'My name is Henrick Baines, Father to Elizabeth Baines, who married a distasteful young man named Robert Shelton.'

Finn felt the life drain from him, unable to struggle anymore he tried to contemplate Henrick's revelation.

'I see you trying to figure it all out, maybe you'll be familiar with the name, Michael Shelton... My grandson.'

'Michael was my Grandfather?'

'Yes, my great, great grandson!' Said Henrick, winking sleazily and smirking.

Finn felt sick.

'So what if you are? *If* you even are, it's nothing! A few strands of DNA nothing more!'

'It's everything my boy.' Chuckled Henrick. 'Just you being here was the spark I needed. The catalyst to my glorious revival!'

'What do you mean?'

'You gave me the strength to manifest myself, to give an old man some guidance.' Henrick moved away hovering to the centre of the room. 'The old man lit the pyre for me, a pyre that I used a long, long time ago. The pyre was a signal, the cue for my storm to attack.'

'But why, why attack? What has Golgothaan done to deserve this?'

Finn moved to the closest wall, propping himself against it.

'The dead have a penchant for repetition, Son. Whether we like it, or not!'

The teapot had been refilled, the conversation so rampant, Eugene had acquired a mighty thirst. He had kept Father Hogan's attention, who wasn't as yet convinced, but found the story an inventive one nonetheless.

'Henrick Baines had built this village on the crossover of several *archaic tracks*, which are also known as ley-lines. These invisible lines were believed to draw spirits, encourage supernatural occurrences. But this was just the start of his plan. The village was built to look much older than it was, most imagining the older the place, the more likely it was to be haunted.'

'What was the obsession with the afterlife? How could Henrick profit from this?' Asked Thomas.

'That wasn't the end of it... He built tunnels, like veins under Golgothaan, secret tunnels that only he and a few hired actors knew about. He would dress these actors, send them underground and tell them to go to the tavern, the Inn, even the church. They would paint their faces white, sneak in at night and pretend to be ghosts, miraculously disappearing in the dead of night.'

Thomas shook his head, smiling wryly.

'This is bizarre. And you're telling me you read all this, down below?'

'I did, I was lost, close to giving up, until I saw this,' Eugene flipped to the back of the journal, where there was a crudely drawn map of the tunnel system under Golgothaan. 'I used this, this tunnel here led straight to you.'

'My, my, would you look at that,' Thomas leant in, genuinely intrigued, he pointed at it, 'so this is the church, and this is where we are now. No tunnel here though.'

'No not every house had one, maybe this place was built later. Anyway, as I was saying, these pretend ghosts would scare the locals, scare visitors and word would spread. Tourism you see, he had grand plans, Golgothaan as you see it now was only mark one, the village was gonna become bigger, better, and eventually, the *most* haunted village in the world.'

'Why bother, surely the construction of a place like this cost much more than he would ever make back.'

'At first it was money, then it became an obsession. Henrick wouldn't stop there, he couldn't, this village was to become his legacy, money could never buy that. Fake ghosts weren't enough.' Eugene flicked through the pages. 'It gets a little sketchy from here on, but from what I've read, the actors were the first to go, murdered by Henrick. Loose ends you see, he couldn't have them spreading the truth. Then one day, a murder took place in the Ashen Maid, and a plaque was laid in memory of the person. I'm sure you've noticed, there have been a lot more plaques laid since.'

Father Hogan nodded.

'I've never really thought about it, I don't care for such things, but I'll admit it, there are a lot.' He sipped his tea, grimacing because it was cold. 'I always thought this village was older, that amount of deaths seemed normal to me, assuming Golgothaan is four, five hundred years old.'

'But it's not.'

'So you and Mr. Baines say, but you haven't proven anything to me yet, just told an interesting story. Don't get me wrong Eugene, I have enjoyed this, but then I often do enjoy fiction.'

'I know that it's true, because of what I did... I caused this, all of this.'

Eugene found a particular page in the journal, then handed it to Thomas to read.

'*It matters not, when the pyres lit. If you run, or hide, or stand, or sit. A bitter wind, pass plain and clod. You're on your own, no hope, no God...* What is this?' He asked.

'Prophecy!' Blurted Eugene.

'My storm stirs!' Said Henrick, looking to the door.

'The storm... What is it?' Asked Finn.

Henrick appreciated his grandson's interest.

'I call it a storm, but it's a collection, a collection souls, owned by me. When I was alive, I murdered many, some by my hand but most by my will.'

'You're a monster.'

'Perhaps. I never really enjoyed it, such a messy business. What does a man with means do, when he doesn't want to do something himself?'

Henrick stared at Finn, waiting for an answer. It never came.

'You hire help, stupid boy. The storm were once a band of mercenaries. Mercenary is a nice word for murderer. These men were bloodthirsty, ferocious, inhuman. You think of me as a monster. The storm, that is the thing of nightmares. They would hide out on the moors, wait for my signal, the burning pyre, then they would swoop down, and kill everyone in Golgothaan.'

'Why? Why would you do this?'

'Honestly... I don't remember.' Henrick scanned the room. 'I had a journal here somewhere, that Eugene fellow must have taken it. I will have to catch up to him later. You see Finn, the dead don't remember things like the living do. Some things remain, while others are a blur. We know to act, that we know. The storm only acts, their will is mine... A debt in life, is a debt in death.'

'You don't know *why* you killed Rufus, or the others, you just did it?' Growled Finn.

'Do you ask the wind to slow down, change direction? It does as it does.'

Finn stood up, nervously, curious as to how trusting the entity was, after all, he was family. As he took a step, Henrick reacted, but not to him but the sound behind the heavy wooden door. Finn fell back against the wall.

'It seems, someone is leaving Golgothaan... This will not do.' Said Henrick as he swelled, his form becoming amorphous once again.

A sound like rushing water could be heard on the other side of the door as the mass of shadows left, flushed down the tunnel, acting out Henrick's silent command. This was an opportunity for Finn, now that the way was clear, he was willing to risk his life rather than remain any longer in the catacomb. It was a matter of time before his host would snap. Henrick's mind was as unstable as his form, that would distort when his emotions ran high.

Finn inched his way, casually towards the door watching his captor who seemed to drift aimlessly across the room. Henrick seemed to be with the storm, seeing through its many eyes. Finn felt the iron loop handle, gripped it firmly with his hand behind his back, then waited for his chance.

'It's difficult to accept omniscience, and not accept the fact that you are a god.' Bragged Henrick.

Confused by the statement, Finn took it as his cue, flipping open the door and fleeing, running aimlessly down the tunnels. Henrick didn't react immediately, he took his time, watching his grandson sprint ridiculously. The study was Golgothaan's heart, the tunnels, its arteries. Henrick Baines knew Finn's every step, could feel his every breath, each tremor of the boys pulse.

He ran till he breathed hot coals, slipping and sliding but enduring nonetheless. Finn took little time to notice the skulls in the wall, though as he breathed heavily, the smell of rotting flesh hit him hard. A chilling breeze followed him, it carried a whisper with it.

'Are you quite finished?' It asked.

Ignore it, he thought, carry on, this is your only chance. The breeze was in front now, carrying on down the tunnel, well ahead of Finn. Another voice was in the tunnel, a voice that Finn recognised. It was coming from the mud wall and it stopped him in his tracks.

It was Rufus, whose face was protruding from the dirt. He was alive, calling out to his friend, desperate for help. His face was one of many fresh faces in the morbid mosaic, but his was the only one moving, struggling for breath.

'Help me, Finn!' Begged Rufus. 'Get me out of here.'

'You're alive, that fucking liar, I can't believe you're here.'

'Get me out of this shit, Finn, I can't breath...'

He wasted no time, scooping mud by the handful, starting around his friends head.

'That's it, Finn. Keep digging.' Said Rufus, his head wriggling in the hollow.

As Finn loosened the dirt, its structure fell apart, and Rufus was freed. Finn noticed the head roll free from the dirt, expecting a body to follow it. Instinctually he caught Rufus who now rolled around in his arms, laughing hysterically. There was no body, just a head. The hollow of Rufus' neck was still wet, clogged with mud that oozed out. Finn dropped his friend, horrified, the severed head slapping the dirt by his feet, still laughing.

Finn backed up, finding it hard to turn and run away, though he desperately wanted to. The laughing head kept him there, this terrifying lump of meat and bone was once his friend, and despite the ruse, he still felt the need to help him.

'You wanted your friend, Son.' Henrick manifested beside him. 'Here he is!'

'Don't call me son...'

Suddenly every head, buried in the wall began to squawk the word 'Son!'. Finn covered his ears and dropped to his knees. Rufus joined in, his taunts were more harmful than the others.

85

'I grow tired of this, I have work to do and you are slowing me down.' Growled Henrick.

'So kill me then!' Yelled Finn, trying to drown out the squawking wall.

'You know that I won't, people only invite death when they don't think it will come.'

'I don't know what you want from me!'

'Just being here, is enough... Son!' Henrick smiled.

Father Hogan had wondered to the living room window, staring out at the sky and pondering Baines' journal. Eugene still sat at the dining table, perusing the book, stating whatever snippets of information he could find, and accepting them all as gospel.

'The mercenaries wiped out the village, every man, woman and child. Henrick had hoped that this much bloodshed, this much misery would leave its mark on the earth. If there were such things as ghosts, then he was going to prove it.' Eugene shook his head. 'One hundred and twenty-nine, dead, for the sake of an experiment.'

'That is terrible.' Added Thomas.

He flicked to what seemed to be the last page of the book, the scribbles ending mid sentence.

'This is the last thing he wrote, *I don't know how, but I will get rid of the men tonight, they have served their purpose.*'

'That's it? The end.'

'I'm afraid so... However Henrick did it, I believe that the mercenaries are back from the dead, acting on his behalf. I've seen them, an ungodly cloud of shadows, its presence is the purest evil, I felt it, I know. You don't have to believe me, tonight there will be no choice but to face it.'

Thomas turned to face the frightened man at his table. It was hard to remain stubborn when so many seemed to believe. The story Eugene had read did jar him, though he would never admit it. Turning back to the window, he looked out onto Golgothaan, he noticed an ominous storm cloud on the horizon. It was moving fast, moving with purpose, and its unnatural animation stirred further doubt in Father Hogan.

Below the clouds, another storm was brewing; The villagers were gathering, riled and brandishing weapons of differing intimidations. Most were brooms sticks, rolling pins, kitchen knives. Held by people who have never known violence in their quaint little lives.

'This doesn't look good.' Said Thomas, 'This doesn't look good, at all.'

Still no phone reception. Stacey had been driving for twenty minutes and was yet to pick up a single song on the car radio, just irritating static. It must have been the moors, seemingly endless pasture and not a telephone mast in sight.

There was one road to Golgothaan, one road in, the same road out. Crudely laid, and wide enough for just one car, it was clear that it didn't get much use. The blue skies ahead were a sure sign of safety. There was a tugging in her gut, pulling at her the further from Golgothaan she got. She was sure it was guilt, leaving Jessica as she did, her selfish abandonment which to her made complete sense. Jessica was given a chance, she asked her over and over to leave, but she wouldn't. If people were dying, why should they both risk death for the sake of a stranger, and a strange little village.

Checking her mirror, she noticed the dark skies behind, that seemed to bleed into the blue, tainting it with ominous dismay. Stacey put her foot down, driving faster than she ever had before. There were no signs, no police, who was to stop her, escape was her only priority now.

Storms, at their fastest, usually travel at around sixty miles per hour. Stacey was clearing ninety, according to the speedometer, yet the storm was catching up to her. The ground was darkening, the luscious greens becoming dull, her foot was pressed flat to the metal but it didn't seem to matter. Soon the first drops of rain hit her windscreen, each patter filling her with dread.

It didn't take long, the sprinkling had become a downpour, the breeze had become a gale, the shade had become darkness. Stacey was driving blindly, the headlight's beam cut short, showing only rain and some of the gravel on the road. It was hard to believe just how beautiful the moors were, only a few moments ago.

She endured, hoping to spot some kind of civilisation; a lamppost, a road sign, anything. Anything would have given her hope, just the thought of another person having existing where she was, would bring her some comfort. Tears began to stream down her face, as delicate as she was, this was too much for her to handle.

'What do you want!?' She screamed, over and over.

As her throat became sore, she wheezed her plea, begging for answers.

The water on the glass blurred everything, but a speck of light was visible in the distance. She was awash with relief as she spotted another light, then another. The lights filled her with their imaginary warmth, it was clearly life, and it was approaching fast. As they came closer, the storm began to let up, clearing slowly, revealing more of where she was heading.

Stacey slammed down on the brake, her tiny car swerving in the gravel. The view ahead, once the promise of salvation, had become the horror she'd fled desperately from. She couldn't understand how, but the storm had turned her around somehow, obscured her view and led her straight back to Golgothaan. Stacey shrieked at the top of her lungs, both furious and devastated she pummeled the steering wheel and anything else within reach. She could see the gathering mob in the street, but refused to take a closer look. She spun the car, flinging gravel into the air, and sped away from the village once more. Refusing to give up, the storm wasn't going to win. As long as she had fuel, she would keep driving.

'The weapons will do you no good!' Yelled Lucille. 'Trust me, the church is our only hope.'

Never had so many hung on her every word, an entire mob had formed around her, they clung to her for hope. She had survived an attack, the others hadn't. Nearly every citizen of Golgothaan was there, all except for Father Hogan and a few that were yet to surface. They were all gathered outside the Scarlet Lodge.

'If it's all the same Lucille, I'm gonna keep ole' Gladys with me.' Said a robust man, brandishing a double-barrel shotgun.

'You will cause more harm than good, Patrick.'

'Still, sister...' Said Patrick, his grip refusing to loosen on the barrel.

'Look, what use are these *tools* against the undead. God is our only hope now. Our Lady on the Moor.'

Lucille pointed at the golden cross, high above the rooftops.

'She's right.' Said an elderly woman.

The rest of the mob began to mumble in agreement, nodding their heads. A few raised their weapons and cheered.

She may have been in over her head, the mob was beginning to take on a momentum of its own. Lucille had knocked the pebble downhill, now there was no stopping the rockslide. As riled as the crowd were, one girl was not so enthused. She stood still, on the edge, distraught and seemingly lost. Lucille recognised her; she was one of her guests at the lodge.

'You my child,' She called out, gesturing towards Jessica, 'come forward, please.'

Lucille had adopted a new tone, a new attitude. Confidence had brought out another side in her, it reminded her of the attention she received as a beauty in her youth. Now she annunciated, picked her words carefully, and begun to enjoy to sound of her own voice.

Jessica was hesitant, but failed to resist the eyes that now lay upon her, they beckoned her forward, to leave discreetly was impossible. She meandered the crowd, slowly making her way to the front.

'Where are your friends? The coloured boy, where is he?' Asked their newly appointed leader.

Jessica shook her head.

'I don't know, they're all gone,' Her eyes became wet. 'They have *all* left me.'

Lucille acknowledged her sorrow.

'My child, come here, you're not alone. Your friends saved me, I am indebted to them. That means, I'm indebted to you.'

Jessica didn't want this, the only thing she wanted was Finn. She scanned the faces in the mob, darting between each set of prying eyes. Some offered her smiles, others nodded, while some were worryingly indifferent.

'You don't owe me anything,' Said Jessica, 'I just need to find my friend, I need to find Finn.'

'Was he taken by the storm?'

Jessica nodded.

'Then you must join us, our loved ones will be returned.' Lucille clenched her fist, looked to the crowd. 'We will demand it!'

The mob cheered, the sudden outburst rattling Jessica who stood motionless in an animated crowd. Lucille moved towards Jessica, placing her arm firmly around her, pulling her as she begun to walk up the street. Before she could resist, the crowd had her in its current, the mass moving as one towards the Lady on the moor. The commotion was deafening, the pace frantic, and in all the confusion Jessica heard a reassuring whisper. Lucille held her close and spoke into her ear.

'Don't worry child, I won't let anything happen to you.'

The words were a comfort, after her friend abandoning her and Finn's abduction, she needed this. It was easy to get lost in the warmth of it, the unity of the village that had invited her into its fold. She was going to find Finn, this she believed, and if the storm that gathered above Golgothaan was the evil that had taken him, then it was going to come back for Golgothaan's people. It made sense to stay together, stragglers wouldn't stand a chance.

There was a knock at the door, several heavy handed thuds. Father Hogan knew who it was, he'd watched the mob approach, discreetly from behind the net curtains. Eugene sat up straight, unsure as to their purpose, but wary nonetheless. The priest took his time, exhaling with defeat as he shuffled to answer their call. He could hear their voices, their agitated tones, their impatience, through the wood of the door. He took a little pleasure in making them wait.

He loosened the bolt, turned the knob and inched the door open, letting the mob see only a sliver of the rectory inside.

'Can I help you, Lucille?' Asked Thomas, wryly.

Lucille was standing tall, holier-than-thou, her mob waiting impatiently behind her. Her stoic disposition implied power, it unnerved Thomas to see her this way.

'We need the Lady on the Moor, Father.' She asked, humbly.

'Why do you need it, Lucille. I'm afraid that it is locked for the day. The approaching storm and all.'

'The approaching storm *is* the reason.'

'Well, I suggest going home, locking your doors, keeping a few candles nearby.'

'We need the church, it is our *only* sanctuary.'

She didn't get aggressive, her mob did that for her. The largest of which was Patrick, whose trigger finger itched.

'I can't let you have the keys Lucille, I'm sorry.'

'The church is not yours to keep, Father. It is Golgothaan's... We *are* Golgothaan.'

'That's not strictly true, Lucille. You may have these people in the palm of your hand, but that holds no sway with me. I'm going to close this door now,' He said firmly. 'I'd suggest that you all go home.'

Thomas nodded his head sincerely and closed the door to, the wood bounced as it hit a large boot that was wedged against the frame. It was Patrick's, who took this opportunity to slide Gladys down the woodwork until it was pointed at Father Hogan's face.

'The keys, Father.' He said, gruffly.

This was a situation like nothing he'd faced before. He couldn't approximate it to anything he'd ever experienced, it was a moment that had put every other experience in perspective. A lifetime of servitude was at the mercy of a simple clench of Patrick's finger. He suddenly, in that moment, felt foolish, and as he stared down the barrel of the gun he wished to keep his little life more than anything else.

Lucille wasn't happy about it, in fact it made her queasy, but Patrick had made the move, and it was a sure way to get the keys, to get her people to safety.

'I'm sorry Father, I didn't want this.'

Thomas didn't speak, he just trembled like a cold, wet dog. Lucille, raised her hand and gently pushed Gladys to one side. Patrick hesitantly lowered the gun and gave Lucille a wounded look.

'The keys... Please.' She whispered.

Thomas wheezed, fearing that another palpitation or two would bring on a panic attack. He was a man of peace, this was not something he could ever deal with. The priest stumbled into the living room, reaching for the keys on the side, taking a moment to check on his guest, hoping selfishly to share the ordeal with Eugene.

He was shocked to see an empty chair, Eugene was gone, and so was the journal.

Lucille had followed Thomas, and Patrick wasn't far behind.

'You are coming with us, Father. I care for your safety too.'

He didn't refuse, he just did whatever to crazy lady, and the big man with the gun asked of him.

Jessica had stood aside, watching the crowd impose themselves on the rectory. Then she watched the priest - who looked like a shell of who she'd met earlier - lead the group to the large, decadent church doors. His shaky hand found the key hole, eventually, and he unbolted the door. Several villagers heaved the doors open, allowing the others to trickle inside.

Lucille approached Jessica, ensuring her that she'd not been forgotten, then she gently ushered her in. Thomas was the last to enter the church, now feeling like he was responsible for its safety, hoping that his presence might detour some of the mob - those that were not usually church goers - from disrespecting the Lady on the Moors. He may have questioned his faith when faced with a face full of buckshot, but his church was something he would always cherish.

The heavy doors were slammed shut, Patrick pushed one, while the other was pushed by an old man with large grey mutton chops. The door was locked tight with the big brass key, that Lucille then put in her pocket for safe keeping. She took a casual stroll down the aisle, a subdued smile on her face. She couldn't let the villagers know that she was enjoying this, her moment. Lucille admired her surroundings, marveled at the murals, and was reassured that this was truly God's house. No evil could touch them here.

The rumble of thunder could be heard, the architecture of the church amplifying it, the villagers feeling it in the soles of the feet. The beauty of the stained glass was muted, the light outside gradually dying. The people of Golgothaan had gathered in their supposed sanctuary, and now stood aimlessly, waiting for their newly appointed leader to take responsibility for them all.

The pulpit was as good a place as any to make a speech, Lucille had acquired a taste for it. Thomas watched her climb the few steps and shook his head at the hypocrisy of it, the woman who had ridiculed him earlier for preaching was now walking to her stage, and loving every minute of it.

Some were sat in pews, others were pacing nervously. Some were even hugging and kissing, those that had loved ones left to care for. Lucille cleared her throat and caught the attention of her audience.

'Now, we wait out the storm.' She said, her voice carrying in the hall.

Most acknowledged her words, settling as if they were in a shelter, while others gripped their makeshift weapons, their adrenaline refusing to let go.

'Some of you still seem, agitated,' She said. 'You need not be, this is God's house, the Lord will protect us here.'

'How can you know?' Asked someone in the crowd.

'Faith, friends. What comes for us is evil, the purest kind. It has no place here.'

'I want to believe you, I really do,' Bellowed Patrick, 'but we should be prepared for a fight in any case!'

The more timid of the gathering recoiled, while some agreed with a murmur.

A female voice came from the back of the hall.

'You can't fight it... It will kill you all!' Yelled Jessica, who had been sitting, quietly, close to where she and Finn had been sat the day before.

'How do you know?' Came another voice.

'Because I've seen it with my own eyes, it took my friend in a second,' Her lip began to quiver, 'he couldn't fight it, you can't fight smoke!'

'We can try!' Said Patrick, raising his gun.

'People, it will not come to that, we are safe here...' Said Lucille.

She was cut off by Thomas, who approached her slowly.

'Are you sure, Lucille?' He said, smugly. 'How can you be so certain?'

'Surely you believe it, Father?'

'I don't believe any of this, I believe that your fear mongering has turned a peaceful village into a vicious mob.'

'There has been no violence, Father. This is why we are here.'

The priest shook his head in astonishment.

'I had a gun pointed at my face!' He growled, turning to see Patrick, who was clearly ashamed.

'That was a mistake, he would never have used it.'

'Well that's okay then!' He said sarcastically. 'A gun is a gun, Lucille, I feared for my life whether it was a *mistake* or not.'

Thomas was red in the face, his temples pulsing. He'd never felt this angry before.

'I don't believe in ghosts, not the way you all seem to, but if I was to believe the stories, believe in the killer storm that's coming to wipe us *all* out...' Thomas had made his way to the pulpit, sharing the platform with Lucille. 'Then you should know, a little faith... *Won't* save you!'

Father Hogan's words seemed to encourage the storm. It rattled the heavy doors, wobbled the stained glass, whistled through every crack. The congregation moved, anxiously to the centre of the hall, the stone walls seeming frailer than before as the force outside grew more and more aggressive.

'It's okay.' Yelled Lucille. 'Remember where we are.' She moved down to the aisle, trying desperately to console everyone within reach. 'Try to remain calm. Try to keep faith.'

Thomas remained at his pulpit, waiting for the wind to settle, convinced that it couldn't get any stronger. But it became fiercer still and anticipation kept him there, kept him motionless. How much more could the building take.

When the villagers were sure that the church was about to be uprooted and taken into the air, it stopped. The winds ceased, all that was left of its mighty roar was a slight ringing in their ears. The gathering looked at each other, confused. Some forced a smile, though the tautness of their terrified faces made it difficult. The more naive of the group began to sigh with relief, some even let out a timid laugh. Thomas wasn't convinced, more astute than the others, he realised that the only way a storm could cease so suddenly, was if they were in the eye of it.

Lucille wore the biggest smile of all, looking up to the ceiling and holding her hands together, thanking God. She didn't thank the heavens for her people's safety, but for the sake of the trust that so many had placed in her that was now justified. Lucille next looked to

Thomas, ensuring that he noticed her, hoping to see a glimmer of shame in his face. He showed no such emotion. Amongst the commotion of the celebrating crowd, the priest gave a very silent shake of his head, Lucille watched him, confused.

The silence was broken by a deafening wail, a thousand unpleasant tones all at once as the church organ played itself. It wasn't a tune, it wasn't even a note, it was a terrifying scream. Each pipe an agonised throat, crying with everything it had. It was debilitating, causing everyone to cover their ears and seize up.

Thomas had received the brunt of it, being so close to the organ, he fell to his knees and writhed, screaming though he couldn't be heard over the disharmony. Lucille watched him - blinkered by her raised elbows - and could see his open mouth, wanting desperately to help him. Something else begged her attention, something that could move discreetly thanks to the chaos. A slab of stone was tossed upwards from the floor, then something slithered out from the back of the hall, behind the pulpit and behind Thomas. It was a serpent-like shadow that crept out from a hole in the ground. Lucille called out to Thomas, waving her arms despite the earsplitting shrieks that begged her to place her hands back against her head. It was no use, it was too late, and as the shadow had collected underneath the priest, she knew that even God couldn't save him now.

Thomas stood up, shakily, and felt his footing shift, the ground beneath him was soft. As the shadow begun to swell below him the organ stopped screaming. Lucille's pleas could now be heard, directing everyone's attention to the slowly levitating priest. Thomas didn't realise it was the storm at his feet, he didn't know how to comprehend the pulsating shadow below him. He was being raised, slowly into the air, arms outstretched, and everyone left in Golgothaan was there to watch him. The gradual ascent gave him plenty of time contemplate his death, it was certain, he and everyone else knew it. The storm had him and used him as a show of its power. There were no tears, not from the crowd, they were in awe of it, tears may have caused them to blink and miss something.

Thomas was now high in the air, a column of whirling smog below him, his feet tight together, his hands held out, mirroring his lord on the cross. He could do nothing but pray, rolling his head as he mouthed silent words. The column spun him, showing him the spectacle that was the stained glass window behind him, the window that he loved so much. A single tear rolled down his face as the beauty of it allowed him one last defeated smile. The storm had proven its strength, shown the villagers the futility of their defiance, but it wasn't satisfied yet.

No sooner than Thomas' prayer was over did the monster fling him into the window, whipping at it like a giant cobra, the priest's head smashing through several panes. He began to wail, blood trickling down his brow, hastened down his face by the rain outside. He hung there for a moment, his head outside and his body still in the church, suspended by the cloud and the glass at his chin. The cloud moved quicker now, pulling Thomas downwards, sliding him down the window, shattering and splintering the glass as he went. Each shard sliced at his throat, the further he fell, the quieter his screams became as his windpipe and vocal cords were severed. By the time he'd reached the ground there was no give in the man's neck, as his head detached, leaving his decapitated body to lay on the ground of the church, spouting fresh gore.

The rain and wind rushed in through the newly made opening. The glass once stained with so many colours was now primarily red, slick with Thomas' blood. The witnesses to the horrifying display were lost. Everything that Lucille had told them was wrong. The storm slithered nonchalantly out of the window leaving the flock to marvel at its handiwork. They were no safer here than in the street, the storm had made them well aware of that. Lucille sobbed, mourning the man that she had ridiculed, devastated by his end, the indignity and the injustice of it. She couldn't imagine a worse death, or a more undeserving victim.

It seemed that fuel was never going to be an issue. The adorable little car that Stacey had loved so much, had become a beaten up mess. The unrelenting barrage of flying gravel and pot holes had finally killed it. All but one of the tires were flat, the windscreen shattered, lights busted, and as she had made her fifth unintended return to Golgothaan, the car rolled to a gentle stop, before sputtering and dying. The storm had won, there was no escape. It would find a way to bring her back no matter how determined she was to leave.

She sat in her car, that now rested metres from where she'd originally taken off. The rain and wind outside had found its way in through the shattered windscreen, the comfort and safety she once felt inside was cruelly taken from her. Stacey had no choice but to find shelter, though she was devastated enough to just sit there and accept death. But then death at this rate would be a long, painful one, as the storm did little but chill her, obviously preoccupied with somewhere, or someone else.

Golgothaan was small, she could run for the Scarlett Lodge, but the horror that sent her fleeing in the first place had been there, she couldn't risk facing it again. In her short visit she had visited just one other place, the Ashen Maid, and it was sat, quietly beside her car. Now, as she left her car and became saturated by the downpour did she regret not grabbing her clothes. She was chilled to the bone, her thin vest top and cotton bottoms providing no protection from the elements.

First she tried the front door, below the eave with the sign that read *mind your head*, she was short enough to ignore it. The door was locked tight, there wasn't a chance that she was going to get in this way. With the chaos of the storm and the apparent desertion of the tavern she was sure that nobody would notice a broken window. Searching, near blind, on the rain-slick ground she found an ornamental flower pot. The plant is surely overwatered by now anyway, she thought as she heaved it through the biggest, lowest window she could find. It shattered, but the sound of it was muted by the thunder outside. She batted away any remaining glass with her hand wrapped in the bottom of her vest top - she'd seen people do this on television - then she climbed in.

Stacey was torn; thankful to be out of the rain, but resentful that she should end up back where she had started. It was a matter of time now. The storm would run its course as all storms do, and she was going to hide until it had. Rufus' car was still in the gravel patch, and she was going to try and take it. She didn't know how to start it without the keys, but she was going to try nonetheless. Nothing was going to keep her in this godforsaken town.

The tavern was a different place in the dark, and with no one else to share it with, it had adopted an eerie atmosphere. There didn't seem to be any power, but the lightning flashes from outside lent a glimmer to the bottles of spirits that hung above the bar. One couldn't hurt she thought, as she imagined the warmth of a Jack Daniels going down the back of her throat. It was a cliché, to drink your sorrows away, but if it was possible, then she had nothing left to lose now but her fear and pain, and alcohol would numb them both.

The church was a different place now, the building had become a mockery. God was not there, how could he be, how could there be room for goodness when all anyone could feel was the evil that had mutilated poor Father Hogan. The hall was electric, the presence of the monster was felt in every pore of every one of them. Dumbfounded they all stood shaking, looking at each other for answers and receiving equally blank expressions in return.

Lucille and Jessica were the only two brave enough to approach Father Hogan's body, they knelt over it, sickened, but tolerant of the gore for the sake of his memory. Jessica held her hand to her mouth, her eyes watery and wide. Lucille's faith had left with Thomas' life, and without her faith, she was nothing. She was useless now as she watched her tears darken Thomas' shirt, ignoring the villagers that were in hysterics, calling out her name.

'What now, Lucille?' Whispered Jessica.

Lucille didn't reply, she just shook her puffy, red face.

'We aren't safe here, we aren't safe anywhere.' Jessica looked up, then whispered to herself. 'I was a fool to stay here.'

'You *were* a fool, child.' Lucille muttered. 'You and your friends, fools to even consider coming to this godforsaken village.'

There was a heavy knock on the doors, the wood warping with the force of it. The sound reverberated, silencing all those inside. There were two more controlled thumps, but nobody answered it. Lucille stood up and looked at the door, no longer sobbing, her face was flushed with anger.

'Open the doors!' She growled. 'It makes no difference now, just let them in.'

Most of the crowd shook their heads in refusal, while Patrick and a few others embraced their weapons, ready for a fight. Lucille took the key out from her pocket.

'I said open the doors!' Lucille started heading down the aisle. 'It's time to end this.'

'We have had enough of your advice, *Looney* Lucille!' Mocked Patrick. 'We're going to deal with this our own way.'

Lucille held out the key, which was snatched away by Patrick. He turned it in the lock. Patrick nodded to the Mutton-chopped man opposite, signaling him to heave open the door closest to him, while he pulled the other.

As the huge doors inched open, the severity of the storm outside was made clear, the sky was dark, only the constantly shifting, grey lining of clouds offered any texture, the barrage of lightning strikes, highlighting their dominating size. Rain fell by the bucket load, the drops like bullets, drowning Golgothaan inch by inch. Lastly there was a small figure; a skinny little man who seemed strangely luminescent, the air rippling around him, implying that he was boiling hot, when he was anything but. Patrick and the Mutton-chopped man were the first to feel the strangers chill, that crept along the floor until it had refrigerated the entire church.

The man stared ahead, eyes deep and dark, his blurred mouth seeming to smile. The rain didn't hit him, the wind didn't ruffle his slick black hair, he was ethereal, little more than a trick of the light. The thin man, like a portrait, was able to look everybody in the eyes at the same time. No matter where they were in the large church, he was looking deep into each of their souls.

The confidence of the bigger, more brutish villagers had been instantly sapped, Patrick included, but Lucille stood firm. Her resentment for the visitor was clear on her face, she refused to show any fear assuming that the monster would thrive on it.

'So you finally step out from behind your storm!?' Yelled Lucille, her voice full of venom.

'Would you prefer the storm, *Looney Lucille*?' Teased Henrick. He looked at the two men holding the doors. 'May I come in?'

'We couldn't stop you, we know that now.' She said.

Henrick moved effortlessly, gliding a few metres into the hall.

'Yes, that is true, I'm glad that you realize this now.' Henrick looked up. 'I *never* invited God into this place you know, this is a theatre,' He held out his arms, 'this is all just stage dressing.'

His presence was felt strongest by those closest to him, it was almost magnetic, pulling only at their guts and teasing their bile ducts.

'Why even show yourself at all?' Asked Lucille, moving closer to the spirit.

'Well, it's not for any kind of truce, if that's what you were hoping for. I have no demands, no needs.'

'Then why?'

'For you, Lucille. To disprove you and your claims. Your faith in your God, this church, it roused me.' He examined the crowd. 'These people are not very happy with you... They're all wondering... *If only I'd ignored that loon's advice, I might be safe at home right now, not herded into a pen, ready for slaughter.*'

His words struck fear in them, the word *slaughter* most of all.

'I did what I felt was right. We were never safe in the village, no matter where we were.'

'Oh you don't know that for sure, but now...' Henrick turned to include the crowd. 'You're all going to die, right here, this very night, and you can thank Lucille for that.'

'This is not her fault!' Yelled Jessica, standing by the dead priest.

Henrick seemed to swell as he spotted Jessica by the pulpit.

'Ah the stranger, an unfortunate trip this has been for you. Golgothaan was once a beautiful place, I should know, I built it. But now... It's overcrowded.'

'Then let us leave!' Begged a woman in the crowd.

'No, no, no.' Chuckled Henrick. 'Where's the fun in that? No, my dear woman, there's no other way now... It's time for a culling!'

His smile was morbidly large, his face distorted as he began to free his grip, allowing his form to lose some of its shape. The crowd were too silent, their despair was held off for a moment as Patrick crept up to the monster, Gladys trained on the its back. He wasn't going to risk it, he had two barrels and he intended to unload them both, at point blank range. Henrick didn't react, he just leant forward, staring at Lucille who was now stood, bravely in front of him.

'I won't kill *you*, Lucille.' He whispered, smiling softly.

The comment confused her, unknowing of the large man behind Henrick, the gun mere inches from his ghostly form. Patrick pulled both triggers, both barrels exploding against Henrick's back. The buckshot passed straight through him, as anyone with any sense might have expected, but then the villagers of Golgothaan were not known for their brains. The unfortunate recipient of both shells was Lucille, who was sent back onto the ground, her chest in tatters. She slid along the aisle, unable to express her pain with lungs full of holes. She didn't have long - seconds in fact - to realise just what had happened. Before any of it could make sense, she had drifted into an endless, oblivious sleep.

Henrick let out an unrestrained guffaw as he turned to face Patrick. He then dissipated, becoming several black wisps of smoke that became nothing in the air. Patrick cursed himself, throwing the gun to the ground. He shook his head as he examined the mess he'd made, the trail of blood leading to a hollowed out Lucille. His idiocy had cost a person their life, and though he would hate himself for it, he didn't have time to hate himself now. Survival came first. Patrick turned and ran, sprinting for the open doors, hoping to leave the claustrophobia of the Lady on the Moors and take his chances on the open street.

Others took their cue from him, fleeing the crowd and following the murderer, this was until the heavy doors swung shut. Patrick was caught between the wood, wedged between the doors making it close at a gradual pace, gently squeezing the life from him. It was clamped onto his chest, his bottom half still inside, his head and shoulders outside. The crunch of snapping ribs made everyone grit their teeth. Patrick tried his best to get a grip of the door, but the angle of his snagged body wouldn't allow it. All he could do was listen to his torso shrink, feeling it first in his lungs, unable to inflate them. In his final moments he watched his insides pour from his mouth as a mush, like toothpaste squeezed from its tube. There was gap enough to trap some of Patrick's flesh, holding him halfway up the closed doors, his legs dangling limply.

This was the first of the slaughter, everybody knew it. The storm had returned, swimming in through the shattered window, circling the hall like a bird choosing its prey. It had become chaos, the noise unbearable. Everyone ran aimlessly, trying to climb to the windows, trying to pry open the front doors despite Patrick's gore. It was futile and everybody knew it.

Jessica couldn't fathom her end, the sensation of death that was sure to come within the next few moments. She'd spent her life trying to imagine it, once or twice in fleeting moments she'd even wished for it, but this was too much. Anticipating her own mutilation was worse than the act itself. Pain was definitive, you learn it intimately. Not knowing was the real suffering.

She watched the tempest, limbs and blood swirling around in a vortex of ungodly shadows. The storm was not happy with just death, it wanted to unify flesh, making each and every scrap indecipherable from the next. Flesh stripped from bones, bones smashed to splinters, organs turned to pulp. This was its art, and it shone today.

Jessica curled into a ball, waiting for her turn, refusing to watch the horrors any longer. She felt damp cold fingers on her, clasping at her forearm. She screamed and struck out, swinging her arms and legs without even opening her eyes. Eventually she was restrained by something far to human to be the storm, slowly she opened her eyes. It was Finn, knelt above her, covered in mud and wide eyed. Clearly impatient he was shouting at her, 'Come with me!' he yelled again and again, barely audible over the dissonance. She couldn't believe it was him, she imagined he was a trap, an illusion put there to cause her more sorrow. Finn dragged her, shifting her with everything he had. Ignoring the chaos in the hall, he focused on just one thing; Feeding Jessica into the hole. She came round, just enough to crawl in on her own volition, where she slid into the dark, welcoming the black. Anything to get away from the new colour of the church. A fresh coat of red.

5

Whether God would ever save Golgothaan remained a mystery, but Eugene had been sure of one thing; The Lady on the Moors was never a church. Henrick Baines had built it, but it was never a testament to God, it was only for him and his ideal. It was part of the village's facade, its elaborateness owed to his flair for the dramatic.

Eugene had slipped out of the rectory as soon as the mob had arrived to see Father Hogan. He knew that they would be going to the church, and he knew that his protestations would have fallen upon deaf ears. While slipping out of the back door he noticed a shovel by the priest's disused greenhouse, he borrowed it and left discreetly.

There was only one thing left now. He was traversing the moors once again, heading back to where it had all began, this time it was of his own volition. If the pyre was the start of it all, then it was only right for its igniter to become its extinguisher. Surely what had released the monster could also send it away.

Determined, he refused to ache. Whatever pain he'd felt was incomparable to the suffering of those down in the village. The deaths of their loved ones, the potential extermination of them all, and it was all thanks to a simple book of matches, and the simpler man who was seduced into carrying them to the moors. He questioned the frailty of his will, his sanity even, to be manipulated so easily by Henrick, who at the time was yet to fully manifest, his powers being little more than a ghostly chill felt by the Ashen Maid patrons.

Ethel's voice was not on the wind today, not like before. It was apparent to him now that it was a cruel imitation, and that his wife was blissfully unaware of any of the trivial matters on earth. Eugene took comfort in this thought, the thought that his beloved had played no part - however small - in the demise of Golgothaan and its people.

His life was of no consequence, these concerns of his were distractions that he had to ignore, and as he noticed the flame in the distance - licking at the skyline - he focused on it. His focus and indomitable march was all that he was now. His body ran on autopilot, like a chicken without its head.

The murk of the tunnels offered some solace, but not much. Finn pulled Jessica by her arm, leading her as if he'd travelled this way a hundred times before. She looked around, then looked at Finn, then examined the dirt walls once more. This was all too much, before she could comprehend one thing, another thing would disorientate her. Finn didn't have to pull as hard as he did, she was complying, but his grip had begun to hurt her, leaving bruises on her wrists.

The pair ended up in the underground study, yet another puzzle, confusing Jessica further. Most of all she found it hard to believe that it actually was Finn standing in front of her, a survivor of the thing that had massacred everyone else so effortlessly. Why would it spare him? How could he have escaped? These were questions swirling around inside her head, a head that was already swimming as she was swung from side to side.

As rough as he was on the journey, when they'd reached the strange room he placed her gently in the chair behind the desk, noticing just how violently she was shivering. As he knelt down in front of her, he asked her if she was okay, she replied with a timid nod. There was no time to waste, Finn had to take Jessica's nod at face value, he didn't wait by her side to be convinced further. He head over to a bookshelf, the one that seemed sturdiest, and swept the books from the shelves, letting them slap onto the floorboards.

Pulling at the wood, he heaved it away from the wall gently, hoping to gauge its weight and portability.

'Are you okay to move?' He asked, dragging the shelf back towards the wooden door.

Jessica could only nod, she was shallow of breath and unable to lend any sound to her lips, no matter how hard she mouthed the words she wished to say.

'We need to get out of here, I'm gonna need your help.'

Jessica stared blankly.

'You're gonna have to carry the other end of this,' Finn nodded towards the shelf that he held up at some effort, 'do you think you could manage that?' He asked softly.

She didn't react, she wasn't sure how to. Her eyes became wet, fresh tears promised to join the stale ones down her cheek. In his frantic state he didn't fail to notice her frailty, he just tried his best to ignore it. If he was going to save her, he couldn't let his wanting to comfort her distract him. He dropped the shelf to the floor and walked over to her.

'Jessica!' He blurted. 'We can't stay here, they'll be back soon.'

He clasped her shoulders and gave her a firm shake. It seemed to bring her round. Jessica stood up shakily, then followed Finn to the bookshelf, grabbing the other end as he'd instructed. Her sudden strength was surprising, the adrenaline that came with fear had proven itself useful.

Finn moved fast, but Jessica held her own. She watched the ground more than the way forward, hoping not to lose footing and throw their momentum out of whack. They were working as a unit, the shelf's weight barely noticeable as it dug into her palms, a pain that in any other situation would defeat her.

The seemingly endless tunnels were indistinct, but the further they travelled, the moister the ground became underfoot. Finn didn't react until he had no choice; by now their feet were soaked, wading through inches of rain water. The tunnels must have sloped here, but it was the way that Finn had intended to go. Tiny streams trickled in from the tunnels along the sides, meeting in the middle to form a lake. The lights at the end of the tunnel were out, suggesting to Finn that the water level was high enough to drown them.

He stopped, forcing Jessica to do so as she fell against the now stationary shelf.

'What is all this?' Muttered Finn as he examined the water. 'We needed to go down there, it leads straight to the pub, straight to Rufus' car.'

He gazed longingly down the tunnel.

'What about one of these other ones?' Whimpered Jessica. 'Why can we go down there?'

She pointed to the tunnel that branched off closest to them.

'I don't know where it leads, we need to avoid the surface. All I know is, the Ashen Maid is downhill.'

'We could swim.'

'We can't hold our breath that long, if the water levels off here, then the tunnel at the other end must be totally submerged.'

'So what now?'

Jessica trusted Finn with her safety, despite her suspicions as to his spared life. Finn looked to the tunnel that she'd pointed to.

'We have no other choice.' He said, as he pulled the shelf, and Jessica with it.

She was truly her father's daughter. Often as a child, Stacey would catch her father knocking back whisky in his den, and each time he would tell her that it was cola. She believed him until she'd stolen a taste. One day, after snooping around, she found his flask and took a swig. That was her first - but certainly not her last - taste of alcohol, though the experience of choking on a mouthful of whisky at the age of eight should have been enough to turn her off booze for life.

Stacey had never liked the taste, ever since her first, but as she sat by the empty bar, swigging straight from the whisky bottle, she couldn't stop. If you were to look at her, you'd never guess just how much she could handle, always so clean and kempt, not like your average alcoholic. She'd always thought of herself as a binge drinker, this term was a much more socially acceptable one.

It was almost too dark to see, but when she could make something out, thanks to a flash of lightning, she would see two of it. It was a strange sensation to be blotto in a room that was so dark and unfamiliar. She found it hard to stay awake, sometimes unsure as to her state of consciousness. This couldn't happen, this much she knew. If she was to fall asleep, who knows who she would wake up to, or if she'd even wake up at all, she had to keep herself awake.

Spinning on the stool, she dropped her feet a little, confused as she heard a small slap. In her drunken state, she'd failed to hear the water that had slowly trickled into the tavern. There was now a foot of rainwater, the glimmer of its ripples made clear as she squinted her eyes. Stacey dropped from the stool, flinching as the icy water hit her numbed senses. Her clothes had dried a little at the bar, and the cold had failed to bother her since her last few swigs.

'What the hell is this?' She muttered, as she waded forward a few steps.

The chill was much more tolerable with a stomach full of whiskey, but even in her state, she contemplated the possibility of pneumonia, frostbite even. What else could she do? She had to wait for the storm to end.

The horror seemed like a distant nightmare now, the booze doing to her what she knew it would. In her intoxicated state she felt strangely safe, untouchable even, as though her fear was all she had to escape from. The monsters seemed ludicrous to her now. It took her a bottle of whisky to see reason. It was all in her mind, she could blame it on her imagination. It was like walking down a hall in a dark, empty house and convincing yourself that there is someone behind you. When you run, your own commotion makes it more convincing, so you run faster and faster until finally you're running for your life, trying to escape your own shadow.

Right now, she was taking shelter, escaping the bad weather and nothing else. The weather, so bad that it was drowning the village, starting at the bottom, the Ashen Maid. Stacey begun to find the situation a little funny, sloshing about in the water. She kicked at it, flinging water at the red walls, soaking the decorations that hung on them. She took some pleasure in this, saw it as some kind of revenge for her situation, being stuck in this godforsaken village that she had grown to despise. The randomness of her kicks became rhythmic, and soon they became a drunken dance.

'Fuck you, Golgothaan!' She chanted as she kicked, each time becoming more aggressive.

She had danced her way sloppily across the tavern floor, enjoying her tantrum blissfully in the dark, away from any prying eyes. The drink alone was not enough for her outburst, it was thanks to the complete isolation that she could let go. If there was a ever a ghostly presence in the Ashen Maid, she certainly couldn't feel it now.

The water was murky, tanned with filth, not that Stacey could see this in the dark anyway, it flowed down the cobbles, dragging whatever dirt it met along the way with it. This couldn't account for all of the filth, unbeknownst to Stacey, most of the dirt was rising from the flooded tunnels below.

Her ridiculous strut across the floor was disturbed as her footing was lost. The last step she took sunk deeper than the last, so deep in fact that she fell. Stumbling forward, she sunk instantly, then resurfaced in a panic-stricken flail. The water was foul, she spat it out as she tried to tread water, inexplicably in the middle of a room that a moment ago, was only flooded a foot deep. She could feel the cold now, a million needles piercing every inch of her, and all in an instant. She was amazed to feel her heart beat once more, to be able to take another breath, she was sure that the shock was enough to kill her.

Stacey had fallen into an open trapdoor, something that had been hidden in the dark, and obscured by the filthy water. She felt for its edges and clasped at them with her long nails, several of which snapped under the pressure, the pain of it going unnoticed in her panicked state. The stock of filth and sewage stung her eyes, but she blinked them clean, just long enough to notice the wooden door rising slowly from the water. There were no hands lifting the wood, no arms heaving it from the water, the trapdoor was closing on its own.

She had to move but couldn't. Paddling her feet did nothing, the strength was sapped from them in the ice water, the booze she had drunk denied her any kind of coordination. All she could do was watch the door close, barely able to muster a whimper with a mouth full of filth.

There seemed to be time to contemplate her life, though the closing of the trapdoor lasted only a few seconds. Her memories worked in reverse, the first being her abandonment of Jessica. After a series of other life events, most seeming so trivial now, her final thought as the door slammed shut was that of a swimming lesson she'd taken as a child. Only six, she remembered it vividly; An older girl holding her head under water for that one second too long. The unnatural feeling of water pouring down her throat, filling her lungs. It was only a dribble back then, this was cascade.

This was not the fire he'd started. The pyre Eugene had lit was merely wood and flame, this was so much more. It was animated like no fire he'd ever seen, moving as though it was a living thing, flailing with many fiery limbs. It convulsed, beating like a huge, excited heart.

The purpose of his journey across the moors was to extinguish it, but this was going to be harder than he'd expected. The fire looked as though it had a will of its own, and if Eugene was to try and kill it, it would fight for its life as any other living thing would. The shovel he'd borrowed was for the dirt, his intention was to smother the fire, to suffocate it. He assumed that water wouldn't work. The wood was wet before, and still it ignited easily. The pyre had also survived the downpour of the storm. Eugene could think of no other way but to choke the life from it.

The dark storm clouds were still swirling above the village, while Eugene and the pyre were under a calm, blue sky. The moors leading off to sea were peaceful, beautiful even, and it was only a matter of time before the storm's eye would be directed at him, and its own heart. He wasted no more time, ramming the shovel into the dirt at his feet. The rain had softened it up, the shovel slid in easily, and as he raised a clump of mud he questioned how fortunate this was. The ground was breaking too easily, nothing had been easy since his visit to Golgothaan.

As a young man he'd laboured like this, working on building sites, lumping concrete into mixers, but his muscles were taught back then. Now they were pathetic slivers of wiry meat, doing everything they could to keep him upright, let alone dig a small trench.

He flung the first clod, his bones creaking as he did so. It slapped against the wood, the fire hissing violently, the flames reacting as though they were in pain. Eugene felt a sudden burst of heat on his face. The fire roared at him, swinging at the old man who was just a few inches from its reach. This was going to work, suddenly he was convinced of the fact as the pyre seemed to be afraid.

Eugene dug until his arms became numb, tossing more and more dirt and aggravating the fire further and further, and as the fire began to shrink, the storm above Golgothaan began to rumble. This was going to work, he was sure of it. All he had to do was keep it up, which for a younger man would have been easy. For Eugene, this could become the death of him.

They were both lost, not just Jessica. Finn had seemed confident, his bravado, clearly forced, but it was enough to rouse her into action. Now they ran aimlessly down yet another tunnel, heading up stream, slipping and sliding as a trickle of rain water slithered underfoot. His logic was to head uphill, hoping that the climb up to the surface would be made easier if the brunt of the work was done on foot.

Exhausted now, still carrying the bookshelf that now weighed so much more, they had slowed, and continued to slow the further they went. The sound of the water was barely audible against the slapping of their feet, but Jessica was the first to notice another, fiercer sound. The dribble at their feet was nothing, the sound that seemed to approach was a whoosh, a torrent of something that grew exponentially.

Jessica stopped, then Finn, secretly grateful to catch his breath. She examined the tunnel behind them, trying to pick out shapes in the dark. Only a few bulbs from the ancient lighting system still flickered, lending not nearly enough illumination to the depths.

'What is that sound?' She asked.

She already knew the answer, she had heard the sound before. She hoped that Finn would offer another explanation for it, one that was not so terrifying. Finn had always been pale, but his face drained of blood was an unprecedented shade of white.

'Come here,' He whispered. 'drop the shelf and get behind me.'

He dropped his end and moved over to her, his breath loud and quavering. Jessica let go at some effort, her nails had been pressed into the wood so hard that they had sunk in. He swept her aside with his arm, moving her behind him, she cooperated as a child would, not fully understanding the actions of their parent, but knowing that they were for the best.

Finn stood strong, his position was that of someone in complete control when he was anything but. It was an act, and before he could convince anyone or anything else of it, he tried desperately to convince himself.

'What are you doing?' Jessica pulled at his arm. 'We need to run, now!'

'You know what it is, we can't outrun that thing.'

'Come on, we have to try!' She cried out.

'Trust me, Jessica.' He said, firmly. 'Please.'

She wanted desperately to run, she tugged at him as best she could but he wouldn't budge. For a skinny guy, when his will was set in stone, his poise was set to match it.

'Please, Finn, you're killing us.' She whimpered.

He shook his arm free, pushed her back a little and turned to face her.

'Trust... Me.'

His words were concise, his expression scarily convincing, and at this point she could see no other option. The monster knew these tunnels, it moved like flushing water, they could never outrun it, even if they knew which way to turn.

The lights in the distance were blotted out as the shadow thundered towards them, making the very earth tremble. Jessica took a few gentle steps back, torn as she moved away from Finn but unable to resist it. The sound of it was deafening, it shook his bones, trembled his limbs, but they remained fixed as best as they could, Finn holding his ground, stubbornly. He wasn't sure what was going to happen, for all he knew the storm would meet them and pass through as though they were wet tissue, shredding them in its wake like a power drill through polystyrene.

Air met him first, the storm forcing it down the tunnel like a piston. It hurt his eyes. The wind made him aware of just how wet his face was, saturated with nervous perspiration. Just metres away, Finn braced for impact, squeezing his eyes shut and cursing himself for his stupidity. He could just about make out Jessica's screams over the chaos.

'Stop!' He yelled, his hand held out for dear life.

Everything was still, all was silent, and Finn was sure that he was dead. It was painless, but then he imagined a death so sudden would have been. He heard his name, yelled out by Jessica, it forced him to open his eyes. The water on his face begun to freeze, his breath became fog, he could be forgiven for expecting to see a tundra before him. Instead there was a wall of twisting, writhing shadows. Parts of it were smoke, others parts were solid, but the sum of its parts would refuse to settle as either. Being this close, he could decipher faces in the dark, cold eyes and cavernous mouths. The warped, vacant faces of the mercenaries hired by Baines, so many vicious souls made one, held together by the sum of their desires. Their aim in life was murder, it was the same in death.

The storm had obeyed him, but it seemed eager to reach across and have at Jessica. Finn inhaled a lung full of chilled air, feeling as though he'd not taken a breath in a long time.

'What is this, Finn?' Whispered Jessica.

His control over the monster frightened her, and whatever trust he'd earned during their flee from the church, was suddenly gone.

'You can't have her!' Snarled Finn, 'Do you hear me?'

The storm rumbled, its vortex spinning faster.

'Go now, leave!' He yelled, waving his trembling hand.

It growled, both confused and agitated, slowly swelling and inching ever closer to Finn who stood bravely, refusing to budge. The longer he stood there, the quicker his confidence faded. Something had to happen, he couldn't hold it together much longer.

'Go!' He screamed.

The monster screamed also, its cry was earsplitting, causing Finn to recoil. His stance was broken, but the storm didn't attack. Instead it withdrew, snapping back down the tunnel it had it come from, travelling twice as fast as it did before.

As the tunnel emptied, heat returned, a heat that seemed to thaw out Finn. He fell to the ground, clutching his chest and wheezing uncontrollably. The floodgates had broken and all the fear that they had held back, took him all at once. 'My god!' He muttered as he tried to steady his shuddering heart. Jessica refused to help him, she just stood back and watched the boy struggle, unsure as to whether she ever really knew him at all.

It was a battle like no other. Eugene was not a fighting man, and to become as such at his age had taken its toll. The fire had held its own, whipping at the old man with its flames, flailing them as spiteful tendrils that would blister the skin as soon as touch it. His face was swollen, his fingers fat, the heat had broiled him.

The pyre wasn't half the size it was when he'd begun, it was struggling against the weight of so much dirt, cordoned by the trenches that Eugene had dug. This battle was his, and still the storm seemed oblivious. Just a few more shovels full and it would be done, he knew this, and it seemed that the pyre had accepted it too. He pressed the shovel into the dirt with his foot, feeling the weight more than ever now. Now that the end was so close his adrenaline had petered out, letting his pain return, tenfold. The blisters were the worst, they stung like nothing else, and he could feel them everywhere.

One more clump slapped against the wood with a hiss, he braced himself for a lash but the fire hardly reacted. He smiled, though it hurt his face to do so. This gave him a little momentum, encouraged now to throw on the last few loads, without a potential blistering. There was not a patch of grass left at his feet, he had scarred the moors, struggling to scrape together another shovelful.

Suddenly he felt a change in the wind, the gentle breeze on the hill had become a gale, and the sunlight that he had been enjoying so was slowly disappearing. The storm knew, it could feel its end and had now turned its eye to Eugene. The shadow had shifted, leaving Golgothaan and moving quickly across the moors. No ordinary storm could move like this; this one was angry, this one had purpose.

'Dig you old fool!' He yelled to himself, trying to get a decent lump of dirt to throw.

The first drop of rain hit his hand, the coolness of it felt strongly against his burns. One more clump slapped the pyre, barely hissing now, only the sound a torrential rain could be heard traversing the moors, desperate to meet him. The last of the natural light faded and only a few licks of blue flame still remained. He buried his shovel once more, sure that this would do it, choke the life from of the fire and banish the monster.

The storm reacted, swirling in the sky, making the very air electric. It sent a funnel down to the ground; a twister that churned away at the dirt, sending clumps of earth effortlessly into the air. It knew its target and charged with everything it had towards him. Eugene, who should have been digging, stood and watched, amazed by the spectacle of it, the untamable rage that one insignificant old man had managed to provoke. It was hard to gauge just how far the tempest was, his eyes were not the best, but he was sure it was close, feeling the pull of it from where he was standing.

Dig! Screamed the voice inside his head, snapping him back into action. The rain was heavy now, the wind bitterly cold, the storm was doing all it could to disorientate him, trying desperately to distract him until it could reach him and tear him apart.

The twister was fierce, swelling as it got closer and screaming with a hundred furious shrieks. He panicked, failing to find a decent clump of dirt he moved to the pyre, he started striking it with his shovel, beating it down with everything he had. A rush of Embers flew into the air, dancing around the shovels blow and dying in the rain.

The fire was pathetic now. It was no bigger than a wounded cat, and Eugene proceeded to beat it as though it were, desperate for its pain to end. Each beat against the pyre caused a bolt of lightning to strike the ground. Each more aggressive than the last, Eugene realised that if the storm's aim was better, he would have been sizzled long ago. The last bolt made the hairs in his ears tingle. The wind was testament to just how close it was now, he was barely able to remain on his feet, feeling his weight lessen as the twister tried harder to toss him into the air.

Thwack! The final blow was stronger than the others, and it was enough to kill it. Luckily this was all he had left in him, but still it was more than the pyre, that was now a pitiable black sludge. The storm didn't scream, it didn't have time for a death rattle, as soon as the last flame died, the clouds dissipated in an unspectacular fashion. It was as though the blue sky had easily overpowered it. Like it could have at any moment but waited for Eugene to make the invitation.

Golgothaan was its sunny self once more, the beauty of the village, that was easily forgotten in all of the horror, had just as easily returned as Eugene admired it from afar. It was hard to believe that anything could have been so dark, now that the sun gleamed so gloriously. The old man fell to the ground, sitting as best he could despite all of his aches and pains. Laying back, his head on the moist grass, he felt like he could sleep for the last of his years.

The tail end of their journey in the depths had been a nervous one, especially for Jessica. All she'd had in the dark was the protection of Finn, who she once might have loved. Everything had changed since their confrontation with the storm. When all he'd asked of her was trust, Jessica could find none to give. They'd met only days ago and suddenly she was made very aware of this fact. Before she was awash in emotions, but the shock of all that had happened in the church, and then the tunnels, lent clarity to the situation.

Finn had taken charge again, carrying the front end of the shelf once more, Jessica taking the bottom, playing along until she was safe enough to confront him. They had reached an opening, a slither of daylight making it through a crack in the planks above.

'Lay it against here.' Ordered Finn, pointing to the steep slope leading to the wood above.

She obeyed, dropping it into the mud and letting Finn adjust it, making sure that it was fixed. It was a makeshift ladder, and Finn was the first to test it out, bouncing on each shelf, hoping that they would hold his weight. The bookcase was old, from a time when craftsman took pride in their work, it was sturdy enough. He climbed and pressed his hands against the planks, pushing against them as much as his footing would allow. They were firm, old but firm, and dust fell through the cracks as he heaved, blinding him temporarily. There was no give, he pushed as hard as he could and all he'd got for his efforts were a few nasty splinters.

'After all this!' He muttered.

'What?' Asked Jessica.

'After all this,' Finn started ramming the wood with his shoulder, 'it's sealed up tight!'

Each blow made Jessica flinch, she didn't trust him, and now saw only the aggression in his nature, it seemed to be magnified. She was probably overreacting, he was acting as anyone else would in such a frustrating situation. The throbbing vein in his temple, the foam that gathered in the corners of his mouth, even the way he cursed had more bile to it now.

'Fuck, fuck, fuck!' He growled with each beat of his shoulder against the planks.

'We'll have to find another way.' Said Jessica, as quiet as a mouse.

Finn failed to hear her over the commotion. In his fit of rage he also failed to notice the shadow that blotted out the light for a moment, Jessica noticed it but said nothing, struggling to say anything loud enough to be heard. Suddenly a bolt was slid, and the trapdoor gave way to Finn. The momentum took him by surprise, forcing the door up and then letting it drop again on to his head, the pain was irrelevant though as freedom was a possibility once more.

He climbed up into the unknown room and darted his head from side to side skittishly, then he reached back down into the hole, hoping to clasp Jessica's hand and heroically pull her from the darkness. When he looked down he saw two wide eyes staring up at him, they glistened as they caught the light. Jessica hesitated, her arms fixed to her side, until Finn waved his hand a little more assertively. She took it and Finn yanked with all he had, she climbed the shelves easily as he pulled her, finally leaving the murk of Golgothaan's underbelly.

Finn slammed the door shut, then helped Jessica to her feet. They both examined the room. It was a large tool shed, grime covered and misty with cobwebs, it looked as though it hadn't been used in years. There were tracks on the floor, carved into the grime, they led to a crate that had been recently moved. It must have been sitting on top of the trapdoor, and moved to allow Finn and Jessica up. Jessica noticed these marks, she also noticed how indifferent Finn was, choosing to ignore them while they were blatantly distinct.

Finn checked through a clouded window in the shed door; it led to an overgrown garden. What was most surprising was the sunshine, it was a beautiful day outside, a complete contrast to the depths they had suffered. The door hinges were rusted tight, but they gave way eventually, letting in some welcomed fresh air. Wondering out into the garden, Jessica wasn't far behind, reveling in the open air and the freedom that came with it, even if they were in somebody's garden with no apparent way out.

'I can see the church over there,' Said Finn, pointing to the spire. 'that means the Ashen Maid is over there somewhere.' He pointed roughly with his other hand. 'Rufus' car is over there too, it isn't far.'

Jessica nodded.

'What's wrong?' He asked.

'Nothing, I'm fine.' She snapped.

She seemed close to tears. Finn, thinking about it, couldn't remember the last time she wasn't.

'Are you sure? You haven't said two words to me since that thing in the tunnel.'

'I am fine!' She stressed. 'I don't know how to deal with any of this yet, and until I'm out of here, I won't!'

Finn nodded gently, his concern for her was convincing, even to Jessica.

'I want to get out of here too, there's nothing I want more. We just need to keep it together a little longer,' He tilted his head a little. 'Okay?'

She nodded, offering a small, forced smile. It was enough to keep his suspicions of her suspicions at bay, and immediately he began looking for a way back onto the street.

The fences were high, but not too high to climb. They could have made it over if the owner of the property hadn't strung barbwire along the top of it. The wires were old and rusted, and despite everything that had happened, risking a snag on one the spikes seemed like a risk they didn't need to take.

Finn tried the back door but it was locked. Peering inside, it seemed that nobody was home, and on further inspection it looked as though nobody had been home for a while. This back garden did not reflect the aesthetic of the homes in Golgothaan. Each seemed to be uniformly attractive, as you would imagine the interior and back garden to be also. This certainly was not the case, this house being the perfect example of just how rotten Golgothaan's core was, no matter how idyllic it seemed at first glance.

'We'll have to break in, cut through the house, and then fingers crossed, the police will show up and save the day.' Jested Finn, coaxing the smallest of fake chuckles from Jessica.

'Wake up you old fool!' Came a woman's voice. 'Get off ya' lazy backside.'

'Ethel?' Blurted Eugene as he awoke.

He opened his eyes to a brilliant blue sky, littered with wisps of white cloud that moved quickly out of sight. For a moment he'd forgotten everything. Feeling the grass tickle his ear he sat upright, witnessing the spectacle of wide open fields as far as his old eyes could see. Waiting for his mind to realign, he could have sworn that his dear wife Ethel was there with him, he was sure that he could feel her arm against his as he slept. Noticing that the moors were his and his alone, he suddenly welled up, as he often would when waking, having to remember the passing of his wife all over again.

'I miss you so much.' He sobbed.

'I miss you too you old fool!' She replied, her voice coming from behind him.

Her voice was sweet music to his ears, he spun like a child, desperate to see her kind, weathered face. Of course she was dead, and he was only ever going to be disappointed, but this disappointment sunk his heart to the point of actual physical pain.

Standing there, with a huge sinister smile on his pallid face, was the being that had brought death to Golgothaan; the man who had built Golgothaan solely to hone such unspeakable horrors. He guffawed viciously at the sight of Eugene's misery.

'You bastard!' Growled Eugene.

How quickly sorrow could turn to rage.

'Now, now Eugene. I allowed you sleep, allowed you to rest a moment. That's more than I allowed the others.'

Eugene examined the form, peered into its eyes, trying to read the creature.

'You act as though your grip on this village is infallible,' Eugene smiled wryly. 'I don't believe that it is.'

Henrick shrugged his shoulders.

'Oh, and why is that?'

'If you were so omnipotent, you would have saved your storm.'

Eugene pointed his hand, smugly, towards the blackened sludge where the pyre once was.

'My pyre!' Mocked Henrick. 'Whatever have you done to my pyre, Eugene?'

His attitude to it confused the old man, surely this was the source of his power, the once beating heart of his murderous attack dog.

'You have no power left, Henrick.'

The monster moved closer, drifting across the moor until its emanating cold sent a shiver down Eugene's spine. He wasn't laughing anymore, his smile was much more malicious, his eyes becoming darker and deeper.

'And, who are you, old man,' Whispered Henrick, with a choir of ethereal hisses. 'to tell me I have no power?'

He wanted to run, but he'd come too far to flee now. Though he stood his ground, he failed to speak, fearing that a breath so close to the ghost, would draw some of its putrescence into his lungs. The monster seemed to wheeze, though surely it didn't need the breath, it was a sound made to intimidate Eugene, and it worked.

'You have been through a lot, Eugene, but don't forget who started this,' Henrick prodded Eugene's chest with an icy finger. 'more to the point, how *we* started this.

Eugene held his chin high, his proud bottom lip quivering as he tried his best to figure out just what was to become of him.

'I *made* you journey to these moors before, remember? And I did that as little more than a shadow. I was a creaky floorboard back then, I could do little more than knock a picture frame from the wall. Yet, seducing you was easy.'

Eugene shook his head, defiantly.

'Yes you stupid old man. I was just a cold spot back then, now I'm so much more.'

'What is your point!' Blurted Eugene.

'My point is, this pyre was not the source of my power, it was just the pebble that started the rockslide. You see, I allowed you to extinguish it, I even wanted you to.'

'Why?'

'Because the dead tend to repeat themselves, Eugene. In life, my band of cutthroats were murdered, the authorities were called, by me, and they had no tolerance for such crimes back then. They were chaotic in life, as they were in death and they needed putting down.'

'So you're a traitor then?' Spat Eugene, hoping to wound the monster.

'Evil is evil, you idiot, being a traitorous murderer carries no more weight than plain ole' murderer. Not in the eyes of most.'

'So if the storm met its end at the hands of the authorities, and as you say, the dead tend to repeat themselves, how will your second end be met?'

Henrick chuckled.

'Same as the first no doubt.'

'I do hope it was painful, I truly do.' He growled.

'Well, Eugene, *you* will never know.' The entity swelled as though it was conjuring something. 'Before, I sent you to the moors. Now, I'll send you to the sea.'

The old man's manipulation took some effort before; he needed to be drunk, and Henrick needed to use Ethel as persuasion. It was effortless now, Eugene bent to the monsters will, acting out Henrick's very thoughts. What Eugene wanted to do now more than anything else was walk across the moors once again, this time heading towards the skyline. He had an uncontrollable urge to reach the water, to feel its sharp, cathartic crispness against his skin. The cliffs that would prevent most from reaching the sea, were never going to keep Eugene away. He would travel there as the crow flies, no veering, no faltering.

As he began his determined march, eyes front, wide and zombie-like, Henrick called out.

'Eugene...'

Eugene stopped and turned robotically.

'You have something that belongs to me.'

The zombie walked over to the monster, then lifted his heavy, waterproof jacket. Tucked into the waistband of his trousers was the journal that Henrick Baines had confessed to all those years ago. He handed it over, loyally, then returned to his definitive walk with a nod from his new master. Eugene always loved a good ramble.

The glass was old, it shattered with the slightest of taps, not like modern glass that would take a good blow or two. All Finn had to do was hit it gently with his covered elbow then reach in and unlock the door. The smell from inside was almost as bad as it was in the depths. It hit them like a punch to the nose, but in a setting like this it could be placed. It reminded Jessica of a great aunt of hers, her home smelt a lot like this. The memory of the stench was clearer than her own great aunt's face, it lingered like the very scent; a mix of urine and human grease.

It was strange that Finn was hesitant to touch anything, considering just how filthy he was. The pair had left the tunnels caked in mud, but still the grime of the house was much to organic, and being in these surroundings seemed to revive some of the neuroses he'd suffered with before. The tunnels were an experience like nothing else, and his ailments were forgotten there, replaced by adrenaline, fear, and now on reflection, a morbid sense of excitement. He enjoyed being the hero, and better still was the hope of surviving as one.

The home was sepia; slick like oiled hair, and along the floors and sides were junk. Heading down the hall to the front door, they passed a living room, where the scent was strongest. He peeked in and noticed a mop of soiled grey hair poking out from the top of an armchair. He imagined it was a corpse, and realised that this would have been something he was afraid of just a few days ago. Now it was nothing. The corpse moved, turning its head to spot Finn and Jessica, who froze as though the old woman's gaze were beaming spotlights.

'Jim?' Croaked the old woman, her voice muffled by an oxygen mask.

'My god!' Blurted Jessica, nearly jumping out of her skin.

'Jim, is that you?'

Finn pulled Jessica close, his touch making her shiver.

'We should leave,' He whispered. 'It's for the best. She has survived this long, if it ain't broke, don't fix it.'

His logic was cold, but then most logic was. Jessica couldn't fault it. She nodded, then watched Finn turn the latch on the front door, gritting her teeth with every click and snap. Pulling open the door, it gave way like a vacuum sealed tomb, letting in fresh air for the first time in god knows how long.

The door was closed gently behind him. They had made it to the cobbled street, and were suddenly reminded of the beauty of Golgothaan as it glistened in the midday sun. It was a lie, masterfully sculpted by Henrick Baines, who given a different moral standing in life, could have benefitted mankind somehow. The peaceful nature of the village, though suspicious, added fuel to Jessica's fire, who begun heading downhill before Finn had even moved away from the old woman's house. Leaving him in her wake, he couldn't help but feel wounded, skipping a little to catch up to her. Now she was outside, her freedom being so close, she didn't need him anymore, and her trust in him was irrelevant. As they paced, she felt safe enough to confront him.

'How did you do that?' She asked.

'What?'

'Down in the tunnel, with that thing... You made it stop.'

Finn seemed hesitant.

'I don't know how I did it,' He lied. 'I just held out my hand, and hoped for the best.'

She didn't know him well, but she knew people well enough to know when they were lying. She offered him a look that chilled him almost as much as the storm did.

'You're lying to me, Finn. That thing, killed them all, everyone of them, mashed them all up like they were in a blender. I saw it take you, and for some reason, you're here. You're still alive?'

'You seem disappointed!' He snapped.

'I don't know what to feel right now.'

Finn took a deep breath, trying to keep pace with Jessica.

'It spared me, but I don't know how to tell you why.'

'You better fucking try!'

'The man, the ghost...' Finn shook his head, finding it hard to comprehend his own words. 'He is my great, great grandfather.'

'The ghost?' Jessica seemed appalled. 'That evil thing, that came to the church? The monster that killed Lucille!?'

'I didn't want to believe it, but somehow, it made sense, when he told me, it was like I already knew.'

'You knew!' She snapped.

'No, not like that, I would never have come here if I knew. I would be a million miles away right now. When I say I knew, I meant, a part of me seemed to align, like a slipped disc, falling back into place. The moment he told me, it was like a sixth sense or something.'

'Oh so now you're a bloody psychic too?'

'No, you're not understanding me...'

Jessica cut him short.

'I don't care how it felt, I care about the fact that the man, I almost fell f...' She swallowed the word, took a breath. 'What I'm trying to say is, you are not who I thought you were. That monster, he shares something with you... And anything, no matter how small, how insignificant it is, it is still too much. Something *that* evil... All it takes is a drop to spoil the reservoir.'

Jessica looked upset, but Finn felt the sting of the words more.

'I'm not evil.' He protested.

Jessica could find no consolation. She was bitter, she hated Henrick Baines for what he'd done, and she somehow felt that Finn was responsible in some way or another. Directly or indirectly, it didn't matter, not to her and the mood she was in. Finn tried moving closer, tried reaching for her hand, but it was cruelly whipped away.

'You have to believe me. I'm a victim too,' He begged. 'this is all happening to me, just like it is to you.'

Jessica gawped, her eyes bloodshot and angry.

'A victim!?' She barked. 'What about those poor people in the church, they couldn't stop it, they couldn't hold out their arms and stop the fucking thing!'

'I didn't ask for any of this, Jessica. I'm still the same guy you knew yesterday.'

'That's just it, Finn. I didn't know you yesterday... Not really.'

The words were pain, each one a vicious prod to his heart. He couldn't comprehend this, even after everything she'd witnessed, he felt that his feelings for her could have survived anything. Clearly this was not the case for Jessica. The trauma of it all had put everything in to perspective. Her time in Golgothaan, a mere few days out of the many in her life, she wished to forget. She wished to forget the village, and everything her nightmarish visit had encompassed. Unfortunately for Finn, this included him. Her family, her friends, her home, these were important. Stacey was important, Finn and Rufus, they were just strangers, as cold as that seemed.

Their confrontation had lasted most of the journey to the Ashen Maid, and more importantly Rufus' car parked beside it. The water was still gathered around the tavern, looking like a reflective pool. Since the end of the storm, there had been no breeze, and the pool was perfectly still, so still that Jessica hesitated stepping into it, fearing that she'd fall into the reflected sky if she did.

Wading through, she hadn't anticipated just how cold the water would be. Though the sun was shining, it hadn't time to warm the water yet. The water level had climbed to her knees by the time she spotted Rufus' car. The gravel car park was raised slightly, the puddle there was not as deep as it was on the cobbles, luckily for their escape, the car might just start.

The next thing she saw, sunk her heart. There should have been just one car there, but on closer inspection she noticed the beaten heap that was Stacey's mini. It looked like it had been fed into a crusher that had run out of power half way through the job. Why was it still here? Was her first thought; next she thought about the state of it, the vision of such filling her with dread.

'That's Stacey's car.' She muttered, saying it to herself more than Finn.

She set off towards it, wading with everything she had, and Finn, taking advantage of this distraction, followed closely behind.

'It's seen better days.' He said as they arrived beside the car.

'What is this? It shouldn't be here... I watched this fucking car leave!'

'Maybe she came back for you?'

'No.' Jessica shook her head, trying to think. 'She wouldn't have.'

Finn had no answers, he stood by, speechless.

'Did he do this?' She asked.

'Who?'

'You know who!' She snapped.

'How would I know?'

He seemed convincingly shocked by the accusation, but how could she believe anything from him now.

She looked around, tried to put herself in her friends shoes, and noticed the shattered window on the Ashen Maid. I would have looked for cover, she thought, where else would she have gone, certainly not the lodge. Stacey must be in there, she'd decided, already heading over to it without warning Finn, who now followed her like a lost puppy dog, desperate for her approval.

There was no sign of her, dead or alive, which Jessica had decided to look at in the best possible light. Jessica had searched the entire ground floor of the flooded pub to no avail, then started up the stairs. It was dry upstairs, surely Stacey would have wanted to get out of the water. Calling out her name and listening for a response, she realised that she'd lost Finn. Torn, she wasn't sure if she was glad that he'd left her, or worried that she was suddenly alone.

Without searching the last of the rooms upstairs, Jessica knew that her friend wasn't there. She checked Larry Mumford's bedroom nonetheless. The room was a mess, and though she was sure that Stacey was not hiding under the bed, still she looked. The building was empty, abandoned. For all she knew, the owner was with the mob in the church, united with all the others as a mess of red slop and ground bone.

Her friend was gone, again. She hated to think it, but somehow it would have been easier for her if she'd found Stacey's body, at least it would have been definitive. Now she was in a state of limbo. Desperate to leave, but tied down because of misplaced loyalty.

An epiphany struck her; Fuck it! She thought. Enough is enough. It was time to look after number one. Stacey left her, and whatever happened after that was through her own choices, she didn't think twice when abandoning her best friend. Standing in Larry's bedroom, she begun to frenzy herself, she started growling;

'Fuck her! Fuck Finn! And fuck this place!'

For her own sake she had to leave, and she had to leave right now. Finn must have had the keys to Rufus' car, either that or he was going to hotwire the thing. That was academic now, she didn't need him, she had feet and enough anger to propel them for a mile or two. That would be far enough for her to slow down, then and only then, when Golgothaan would became a small brown smudge on a horizon of green and blue.

Thundering down the stairs, she didn't care who or what her footsteps might alert. Hitting the water at the bottom with a splash. Finn was there waiting for her, standing in the centre of the room as though he was expecting her. She offered him a brief glimpse, then continued to the way out.

'Jessica, wait!' He muttered, trying his best to yell as quietly as possible.

She ignored him and begun opening the front door. As she pulled it, Finn pushed it shut, forcefully so.

'You can't leave, not just yet.'

'The hell I can't!' She protested, pulling with all of her strength.

'Jessica, please.'

'Move!'

The pair struggled, Jessica's efforts being futile. Once the commotion got a little louder Finn snapped.

'Stop it will you! He's out there!' He yelled, his words stopping her dead.

She scrambled to the nearest window and anxiously examined the street.

The mask seemed to suffocate her more than anything else. It was supposed to help her breath, but it wasn't doing a very good job today. Perhaps the tank needed changing. That was a job for her husband, she wasn't able to lift it. She could never wrap her head around the fact that a full tank of oxygen weighed more than an empty one. Air is air, she would always say. She clawed at the mask clumsily with boney fingers, pulling it to her neck. Where was he? She wondered, then called out his name with what little breath she had.

'Jim!' She croaked.

Ada and James Cross were childhood sweethearts. Now they were ancient sweethearts. Decrepit, their bodies continued to fail, but the last thing that would ever leave her, was the love for her Jim, his face still as young and as dapper as it ever was. He would complain about his baldness, but it was never something she'd notice. If you were to ask her to describe her husband - who was now as bald as a tortoise shell - she would talk about his suave, slick black hair, his fringe combed perfectly to the back to his crown. She failed to see him physically as anything but the man she fell in love with.

'Jim, will you come here!'

'Keep ya' knickers on woman, I'm coming.' Came an equally gruff voice.

'It must be empty again, Jim, 'cos I can't hardly breathe!'

Jim placed his hand on Ada's shoulder and gave it a gentle rub, this was his little way of assuring her that he was still there. Ada's armchair faced the television - which had been broken for a month now - and the back of it faced the living room door. It would hurt her neck to turn, so placing his hand on her like this had become ritualistic. It would let her know when her Jim was in the room, and she didn't have to turn at all.

'Maybe we should get some real air... Fresh air, y' know?' Said Jim.

Ada was confused, she hadn't left the house in months and was surprised that her husband would even suggest such a thing.

'Outside?' She asked.

'Yeah, just a little stroll, like we used to. Down t' the *Maid* and back.'

She looked down at her knees, unsure as to their use anymore, then contemplated the idea in her head. It would be nice, she hadn't seen her neighbours since they stopped visiting. With the new garden fence that Jim had put up she wasn't even tall enough to see over it, unable to spy on her supposed friends. The barbwire was for their protection he'd say, but she hated the very sight of it.

'I don't think I can manage it, Jim.'

'Course you can, Love. I'll be there, every step of the way.'

Ada had trusted Jim for more than sixty years, he'd never led her astray. She was too long in the tooth to change her way now.

'If you think so, Jim.' She cleared the magazines from her lap. 'Gimme a hand would ya?'

After a struggle, Ada managed to stand up, finding it more difficult with the mess that had formed a dam around her feet. Aided the whole way by her doting husband, the sight of the front door filled her with anxiety.

With the slip of a bolt, her tomb was exhumed. She walked out into the blinding white, guided by the familiar hand on her back. Jim's words encouraging her pass the threshold, easing her back into civilisation.

'That's it, Love. Take a deep breath, all the fresh air you could need.'

He was right, Ada hadn't realised just how thick the air that hung in her living room was until she'd taken a step out on to the cobbles. As her eyes adjusted to the light, she appreciated the beauty of the village all over again. It was like her first visit all those years ago, the memories taking her back to when she and her newlywed husband moved to Golgothaan.

'I'd almost forgotten what it looked like out here.' Said Ada, rolling her head adoringly, taking in the scenery.

'T'is beautiful 'ere, I know.' Jim steered Ada, pointing her in the direction of the Ashen Maid. 'Let's 'ave a drink, eh? What do you say?'

'Okay, Jim.' Ada caressed her husband's cold hand that was held at her waist. 'Just the one mind.'

It wasn't until the tavern was in sight that she begun to question this outing. Jim's grip on her waist was gentle, but determined at the same time, and the more she thought about it, she couldn't remember her husband ever being a keen drinker. She considered that maybe he was leading her to a surprise of some kind, but it wasn't her birthday, at least she didn't think it was.

Her memory was patchy to say the least. A few years ago she'd been diagnosed with acute dementia, among her many other ailments that came with age. Ada noticed the shimmering pool around the tavern but her attention was turned to her husband, who was now humming and whispering the words to a song that she had never heard before. It was more of a poem, and though it was unfamiliar, it resonated with her like a deep rooted memory long forgotten.

'It matters not...' He mumbled. 'When the pyres lit...'

'What's that, Jim?' She asked. 'What are you saying?'

She was desperate to know, suddenly feeling like she had woken up on a high wire, her life, inexplicably hanging in the balance.

'If you run, or hide, or stand, or sit...' Said Jim, each word raising the volume of his voice.

A memory struck her, one that chilled her very soul, a memory that should have been the most prominent in her life. She had buried it for her own sanity's sake. It was the memory of when she'd last left her home.

'How?' She muttered.

'What's that, Love?' Chuckled the man, with his strange hand at Ada's hip.

'Why are you here?' She wept. 'We buried you...'

Jim began to chant again, this time aggressively through snarling teeth.

'A bitter wind, pass plain and clod... You're on your own, no hope, no god!'

As the hand at her side became deathly cold, her frail heart was suddenly ready to retire.

'What is she doing?' She muttered, her face so close to the window pane that her breath fogged up the glass.

'We need to go.' Said Finn, tugging at her arm.

'No!' She snapped. 'I will not!'

Jessica pulled her arm tight, loosening it from Finn's grip, refusing to stand by any longer. The pair had watched Henrick Baines, casually strolling down the cobbles, heading towards the tavern with his ethereal arm wrapped around an elderly woman. As the odd couple approached, Jessica recognised the old woman as the person she'd met briefly while escaping from the tunnel.

Deep down she knew that it was wrong to leave her there. Whether she believed that the old woman was safe or not, it was just plain rude to invade her home without so much as a warning. Her mind began to wonder, suddenly she thought about Finn, and his insistence to ignore Ada, perhaps his link to Henrick was a telepathic one, perhaps Finn had planned to let his relative know just where the old lady was hiding all along.

All she knew was that the old woman needed her help, and she was sick of running. It was time to confront the architect. If he was truly all powerful, as far as Golgothaan was concerned, then she didn't hold out much hope of escaping anyway, not if Rufus' car would end up like Stacey's, and not if Jessica would end up wherever Stacey was now.

Finn tried desperately to stop her but was batted away at every attempt. He was almost as afraid of Jessica as he was the monster outside. She opened the front door and stepped out into the puddle on the street, Finn refusing to follow her pass the threshold. She waded towards the monster and his prey, moving faster as the old woman began to struggle. Henrick didn't react to her approach, though he was aware of it, he was enjoying himself far too much, toying with Ada who now struggled futilely in his grip. He begun to lower her head, slowly towards the puddle. This action wasn't slow because Ada fought against it, it was slow because he wished it to be, reveling in the anticipation of it. So rarely did he get a chance to kill with his own cold hands, he wanted to appreciate the moment.

'Stop!' Yelled Jessica, running haphazardly through the water.

Henrick ignored her, Ada now on her knees, her face about to touch the water.

'Take your fucking hands off her!' She screamed.

Jessica was now just a few feet away, and as she prepared to leap, she felt a snag, as though a rope was tied around her gut. It tugged at her intestines, forcing the bile free from her stomach. She could get no closer, each time she tried to approach it was like hitting an invisible rubber wall, that allowed only a little give at the cost of an intense cramp, causing Jessica to gag.

It seemed that Henrick was untouchable, and as Jessica fought desperately to get at him, he refused to react, grinning like a Cheshire cat as Ada's face met the cold water. All she could do was watch and wretch. Screaming with everything she had as she fought against the invisible wall. Ada had no fight in her, her aged lungs let loose a few bubbles of air, and suddenly she was still. Henrick let go of her, letting her drift - face down - like a dingy across the puddle.

Jessica gave up, resting her throat, and bile duct, as Ada drifted closer. She waited until she was within reach, then flipped her over. It was too late, she was probably dead before she'd touched the water, her heart sputtering to a halt. The old lady's face was disturbing; her protruding tongue and bulging eyes. Her loose, blue cheese, skin gave the impression of a body that had been soaking for much, much longer. Jessica had no tears left for her, and as an act of defiance, pushed the body aside. She didn't want to give Henrick the satisfaction, she didn't want him to know just how horrified she was.

'Why?' She asked.

His dead eyes now rested on Jessica, still smiling, it was clear that the thrill of the kill was yet the wear off.

'Loose ends!' He hissed through his teeth.

'Loose ends?' She spat. 'What the fuck are you!?'

Henrick contemplated the question, then smiled smugly.

'I'm an artist, Jessica.'

He proudly held out his arms, presenting his canvas - the village - that seemed to throb as its colour dulled.

'You're a monster.'

'Real art requires sacrifice, child.'

'What sacrifice have you made? The people in this village... My friends, they were sacrificed, and for what exactly? This shithole of a village, in the middle of fucking nowhere!'

'Choose your words carefully, girl.'

'Or what?'

'Or my grandson will lose you, *whatever* promises have been made.'

Henrick looked beyond Jessica, at Finn who had approached quietly. Jessica turned to see him, justified in her feelings of distrust.

'He doesn't have me to lose.' She stated, eyes wide.

'He's the only reason you're not down there with Old Ada, floating like a crouton.'

'You promised!' Blurted Finn, still unsure as to his standing with his dead relative.

Henrick gave Finn a look, one that chilled his bones.

'What do you want with him?' Asked Jessica.

'He has my blood coursing through those veins of his. It's certainly not his winning personality.'

'So you're going to keep him? here, in this place? Why?'

Finn looked towards the monster, equally curious to learn his fate.

'As long as he's here, so shall I be.' Henrick scanned the village. 'He will remain here, start this community once more... There are a lot of bodies to bury, a lot of floors to clean before any tourists can arrive. And girl, this village will thrive once more, fresh meat will come by the coach load.'

'This place? It's a few houses and a church, it's nothing! It's hidden, swallowed by these godforsaken moors!'

Henrick begun to swell, his shadow seeping across the cobbles below his feet, his feet that were now floating a few inches above the ground.

'I warned you, child, told you to choose your words carefully!' He growled.

Finn leapt in front of her, holding out his arms.

'Please, *grandfather*,' He almost choked on the word, 'you promised.' Finn took a moment to think. 'Let her go! Let her leave and I will do everything you ask. I'll drag the bodies to the moors, I'll repaint this whole fucking place if you ask me to!'

He didn't seem to listen, his anger rippling the water at their knees, the buildings around him seemed to warp, bowing as his ethereal fog grew.

'She will spread the word! She will tell the story of Golgothaan!' He yelled, thinking on his feet.

Jessica remained behind him, failing to find any words, but feeling tremendous guilt as Finn offered his life in place of hers. Henrick began to calm at some effort, the wood of the buildings closest creaking as they returned to their intended shape. His feet returned to the ground as his shape returned to its dignified self.

'She will tell them all! Won't you...' He turned to coax a nod from Jessica, who complied vigorously. 'How else will your tale spread? How else will Golgothaan get the fame it deserves?'

Henrick considered the plea, the logic of it making complete sense to him, taking him back to his living days, when he was once a very shrewd businessman. This would quicken the herd, rumours were his bread and butter now and Golgothaan needed to be fed, needed to be kept alive.

'If she means so much to you, let her go. I'll allow it.' He grumbled. 'She had no business being here anyway.'

He immediately head for the Ashen Maid, walking atop the surface of the water, his eyes refusing to meet Jessica's should they rouse him to anger. His sudden indifference to the situation made Jessica feel small, her life in was in his hands and it was little more to him than swatting a fly.

'Thank you, thank you,' Sniveled Finn, 'You won't regret this, I'm sure.'

The monster ignored him, continuing towards the tavern until he was out of earshot. Finn turned to Jessica, clasping her shoulders.

'You need to go, now! While you still can.'

She shook her head.

'But what about you?'

'I have to stay, I have no choice.'

She tried to argue it, but she couldn't. They could both live very different lives, but live nonetheless.

'You know I won't tell, Finn' She furrowed her brow. 'I'll never tell anyone about this place, I won't condemn another soul to this horror.'

'I know that you won't.' Finn tilted his head towards Henrick, who had now disappeared in the tavern. 'But he doesn't.'

Jessica saw something in Finn's eyes that she'd forgotten. She realised that he was a hostage, and was suddenly overwhelmed with sympathy, sympathy for what would become of him, and sympathy for what could have been. If there was ever deceit in Finn's heart, it could never have been through his own choice, he feared for his life just as she did and the only way he could survive, was by befriending the monster.

Finn handed Jessica the keys to Rufus' car.

'Take these and go.' He demanded.

'I'll find help,' Her eyes began to glisten, 'I'll figure something out, someone will come and get you!' She whimpered.

Finn shook his head.

'No you won't! You won't tell anyone about this place, promise me.'

Eventually she nodded, then pulled his face to hers. She kissed him, awkwardly at first, but soon it felt right. She didn't tell him that she loved him, it didn't seem fair to lie to him now.

He rushed her to the car, the pair not saying a word, but both were checking the coast for Henrick. As she hesitantly climbed in, Finn slammed the door shut behind her, sealing her away. He placed his hand on the glass and offered a reassuring nod. It killed her to start the engine but she managed to turn the key. As the engine purred, she had hope, which made her more vulnerable than ever.

As the car pulled away, Finn's world got a lot smaller, so small that he found it hard to breathe. He was happy to see her leave, he knew this deep down but he couldn't help but regret sending her away. Suddenly he was completely alone, it was only human to feel abandoned.

She drove faster than she ever thought herself brave enough to do, her foot pressed firmly to the ground. Swerving dangerously, gravel chipped at the windscreen as she sped, but this was nothing. Jessica would have felt safe in a drag race right now, anything was better than Golgothaan. It couldn't be this simple, to be able to just leave, after everything she'd witnessed, the life distorting horrors that would torture her dreams forever more. She was braced, ready for one last shock, expecting the sky to darken, the storm to swoop in, or to wake up back on the cobbles after a soul-shattering dream.

The further she got and the smaller Golgothaan became in her rear view mirror, it seemed that freedom was entirely possible, until finally she was sure of it. The village becoming quaint once more on the horizon, looking like a postcard. Henrick's reach wasn't this far, surely. She lay off the accelerator, slowing a little, but not too much. Distance from the nightmare offered some perspective, which made it all a little harder to comprehend. Taken out of the moment, it all seemed so farcical, hard enough for her to believe, let alone anyone else if she was ever to spread the tale. Of course she wasn't going to anyway, she'd promised Finn, and this was all she could do for him now.

She rolled down the windows and breathed some fresh air. She never thought she'd breath air this sweet again, the air that hung in Golgothaan was tainted somehow, she realised this now, now that she was away from it.

Her home was only a few hours away, and this was going to have to be enough time to get her story straight. Never one for fiction, never one for lies, she didn't know where or how to start. How could she explain her state, the dead man's car that she's driving, and most of all, the disappearance of her best friend, Stacey. Surely anything resembling the truth would lead to questions, questions that she couldn't answer, not if her promise to Finn was to be kept. Any clues to what really happened would fuel suspicions, and suspicions would lead to investigation. If Finn meant anything to her, then being silent was the least she could do. He would have to suffer the nightmare for the rest of his days, his sacrifice needn't be in vein.

She had survived, whatever came next would be a blessing. No ordeal would be comparable to the one that she faced in Golgothaan.

Resigning to his fate offered immunity in a way. It didn't matter what happened to him now. Jessica had gone - he'd watched the car until it was a dot - and now it was just the monster and him. He dragged his feet to the Ashen Maid, following his dead relative, not knowing what else to do. Entering the flooded tavern he wasn't sure what he'd find, noticing Henrick behind the bar, seeming more human than he'd been in a hundred years. He was cleaning two glasses and urging Finn to sit on a stool with the subtlest of looks.

The monster wasn't frightening, his form as solid as anyone living. If Finn didn't know what he was, he could have believed that Henrick was a bar steward, looking unnervingly natural behind the bar. He took the seat opposite him. Henrick filled two glasses with whisky then slid one to Finn. He was hesitant to take it, noticing that Henrick didn't raise his own.

'Drink it, boy. It's not poison.'

Finn looked at Henrick's glass, wondering why it remained on the counter.

'I'm dead, Finn, I can't drink it. Though I do long for the taste.'

'Why pour it then?' Asked Finn.

'I don't really know, maybe it's symbolic, a toast to our new arrangement.'

'Arrangement? Is that what you think this is?'

'It can be, you don't have to be a hostage, son.'

'I'm not your son!' He snapped.

'Well, there's a part of me in you, we both know it. We both feel it.'

He was right, Finn felt saturated by the entity. Now, as he examined his great, great grandfather's face, he could see a little of his own. It turned his stomach. He took a sip and winced at the taste, hoping that the booze would settle his nerves.

'This is a celebration.'

'This is a nightmare!' Snapped Finn.

Henrick smirked.

'It needn't be.' He held out his arms. 'You are now Golgothaan's ward.'

'Ward?'

'In my stead, yes.'

Finn shook his head and stood up, backing away from his stool.

'This place can go fuck itself, I will have nothing to do with it!'

The glass behind the bar began to rattle as Henrick's mood changed.

'You forget your place, Finn. Don't forget what I am!'

Finn didn't panic, he knew his value now.

'How could I forget?'

As temperamental as Henrick was, he seemed to have learned a little self control as he calmed down. Finn walked to the nearest window, looking out over the village. Resenting the view he turned away, examining the water at his feet. A beam of light found its way to the tavern floor, highlighting something that glimmered below the ripples. It was a gift, and it roused a smile on Finn's face. Suddenly it was all clear, but he dared not dwell on his new plan should his telepathic link with Henrick would give anything away.

Finn returned to his stool and took a swig of whisky. There was no point in fighting it anymore, he was to become Golgothaan's ward as far as Henrick was concerned, but his true scheme required some trust, trust that he would now try and build until his moment would arrived. He needed to be alone and Henrick wasn't going to leave him until he was sure that Finn was onboard.

Finn exhaled, hoping to convince the ghost of his defeat.

'I take it that I have no say in any of this?' He asked.

Henrick didn't nod, he answered with a smile that said more than any words could.

Finn screwed up his face and shook his head.

'How the hell are you here? What are you?'

Henrick poured his grandson another drink.

'I'm dead, Finn. I died with ambition, more than most could ever possess.'

'If this relationship is going to work, I need to know more... How did you die?'

'Most would consider me a coward, but my ambition required complete devotion.' Henrick looked to a beam across the tavern ceiling. 'I hung myself, right there, the ultimate sacrifice for my art.'

As he told his story, Finn could picture it clearer than his imagination would usually allow. He was receiving visions of Henrick's past, the scenes offering more than just images, it allowed Finn to tap into the emotions of the moments too. One of the glimpses was of the tavern, seen through Henrick's eyes raised above the tables and swinging slowly from a noose. He felt the sensation of dying, and Henrick's unwavering devotion to the very end.

Other scenes played in a confusing order. He saw his wife, with child in tow, devastated as she was abandoned, all the while feeling no remorse. He saw the construction of Golgothaan, that built in proud view, and that built in secret, and the overwhelming sense of accomplishment that married both. He saw his first murder, felt the warmth of the foreman's blood on his hands, and the satisfaction that came with it. A sensation of completeness, suddenly forgetting, and realising everything simultaneously. He remembered the trap he'd set, tricking the mercenaries and sealing them in the tunnels below, awaiting the law who would come with only vengeance in mind. Lastly he was back where the visions had begun, swinging from the rafters, the birth of his new ethereal existence.

These were only the few thoughts that resonated with him, out of a lifetime of memories, these were the only ones that he could decipher. Snapping free of what must have been a trance, he awoke to see an empty bar. Henrick was gone without a trace. Finn was more convinced than ever of his protestations to his new title as ward, and it occurred to him that if his grandfather's memories were made clear to him, then maybe his plan was revealed to his captor. It didn't matter anyway.

Finn moved to the object glimmering under the water and lifted it. It was Larry Mumford's shotgun, empty and wet. There was bound to be shells somewhere, he thought to himself, and it would dry in no time. If Henrick existed in his present form thanks to his visiting relative, then all Finn had to do was take himself out of the equation. No Finn, no monster.

Even if Henrick was aware of Finn's intention, there was nothing he could do about it. If someone truly wished to end their life, you couldn't stop them. There's a million ways to die in a quiet little village like this, all you need is a little imagination. If the gun didn't work, if he could find no shells, then he would succeed anyway, just as his great, great grandfather did before him.

The sea breeze carried a scent that returned him to his youth; summer holidays with his parents, as dysfunctional as they were, those were some of the happiest times in Eugene's life. The waves crashed at the rate of his heart beating, slow and steady, calming him the closer to it he got. He couldn't see the water, but every other sense told him that it was there. All that stood between him and it's refreshing embrace was a hundred foot drop.

The spell he was under would carry him only so far, Henrick's power over him was only so much, but it clung to Eugene's need to be with Ethel once more. This was the catalyst to his need to end it all. Reunion is one of the greatest joys one can experience, and when it is with your one true love, there is little you can do to resist it. The wind seemed to call his name using sweet Ethel's voice, urging him to take the last few steps. A part of him seemed to resist, snagging at him, as though the last few feet were through heavy foliage. But this was not enough, with only a step or two between him and the drop.

As he reached the edge he hesitated, feeling something at his back. The sea breeze was met by another gust that came from behind him, then a gentle whisper in his ear.

'Not so fast...' Came the voice.

Eugene came round, waking as though he'd sleepwalked his journey across the moors. Suddenly he was weak at the knees, noticing the potential plummet ahead of him. He fell, swinging his arms to ensure that he didn't fall the wrong way, landing on the grass at his heels.

'Lucky for you old man, you'll live to see another day.' Came a much more familiar voice.

It took a few moments for Eugene's memories to realign, remembering the last choice he'd made that was his own and not those that had been made for him, by Henrick.

'Why didn't you let me fall?' Asked Eugene, looking up to the sky.

'Because you wanted to, Eugene.' Replied Henrick, his voice on the wind.

Eugene shook his head.

'So what now?' He asked.

'Now, you go! Live out the rest of your miserable days.'

Eugene didn't question it, he stood up and moved well away from the cliff. He couldn't understand Henrick's mercy, and he certainly didn't trust it.

'The next town is that way,' The wind pointed him in the right direction. 'You'll find help there.'

Like a dog released into the wild, it took a few nudges to send him away. Henrick, who was unable to find a form so far from Golgothaan, blew Eugene across the moors until the old man had found his own feet and started walking.

He couldn't understand the monster's motives, but he wasn't going to question them. He began to run, a cycle of vengeful thoughts going around in his mind. It was Henrick's biggest mistake to let this particular old man live, Eugene thought. As soon as he'd make it to the next town, he was going to tell each and every soul he'd meet about Golgothaan. Eugene was never going to be satisfied, not until the village was a pile of smoldering ash.

Henrick was a conniving man in life as he was in death. A moment inside Finn's head was all he needed. He knew what his grandson had told Jessica, and his complete faith in her not to speak of Golgothaan. He also knew of Finn's intentions, and even now as he drifted above the moors he could see Finn, searching frantically for shotgun shells, desperate to take his own life. He knew that this was something that he could never prevent, not if the seed had been planted. All he could do now was send trusty Eugene out into the world, and wait. If there's one virtue the dead possess, it's patience.

Printed in Great Britain
by Amazon